'Maybe you [...] **as sweet as** [...] she pointed out tersely, but he shrugged.

'It's a risk I'm prepared to take,' he declared, then drained his drink before looking at her. 'You're going to have to change your name. Talbot will have to go,' he told her, and she braced herself for the first of his demands.

'Why?'

Before answering, Lucas glanced round to make sure Tom was safely out of earshot. 'Because I meant what I said to Tom. The three of us are going to be a family from this point on, and that family will have only one name. Antonetti.'

Amanda Browning still lives in the Essex house where she was born. The third of four children—her sister being her twin—she enjoyed the rough and tumble of life with two brothers as much as she did reading books. Writing came naturally as an outlet for a fertile imagination. The love of books led her to a career in libraries, and being single allowed her to take the leap into writing for a living. Success is still something of a wonder, but allows her to indulge in hobbies as varied as embroidery and bird-watching.

THE MILLIONAIRE'S MARRIAGE REVENGE

BY
AMANDA BROWNING

MILLS & BOON

Pure reading pleasure

First published in Great Britain 2007
Harlequin Mills & Boon Limited,
Eton House, 18-24 Paradise Road, Richmond, Surrey TW9 1SR

© Amanda Browning 2007

ISBN-13: 978 0 263 85360 5

Set in Times Roman 10½ on 12¾ pt
01-1007-54880

Printed and bound in Spain
by Litografia Rosés, S.A., Barcelona

THE
MILLIONAIRE'S
MARRIAGE
REVENGE

PROLOGUE

SOFIE ANTONETTI stirred with a sigh of utter contentment and no inkling that this was the day on which her life would begin to change for ever. A moment later a familiar aroma assailed her nostrils and she sniffed it in. 'Coffee!' she exclaimed with a sultry smile and, opening her eyes, looked up into the fascinating blue ones of her husband.

'I knew there was a good reason why I married you. You make wonderful coffee,' she teased him, and Lucas grinned back down at her.

'Only coffee?' he queried, a wicked gleam appearing in those azure orbs.

Sighing with catlike satisfaction, Sofie ran her hands over his bare chest, delighting in the sensation. Making love with him was the most exciting experience of her life. 'OK, you make love well too,' she added with a coquettish grin, then held him off as he leant towards her. 'But it's coffee I want right now!'

Laughing, Lucas moved back, allowing her to sit up and modestly draw the sheet up to cover her nakedness. 'I know what's under there,' he pointed out as he handed over the mug.

Her eyes flirted with him over the rim as she took a cautious sip. 'I know you do, but unwrapping the present is half the fun.'

'True,' he agreed, standing up, revealing that he wore only a towel draped low around his hips. He retrieved a large box from the dressing table and his own mug of coffee.

'What's that?' Sofie asked curiously, wondering if it was a late present. They had spent a happy few days opening a mound of presents after they had returned from their month-long honeymoon in the Seychelles, but some were still arriving.

Putting his mug down, Lucas made himself comfortable on the bed. 'The wedding photos Jack made up for us,' he informed her, and immediately Sofie set her mug aside and took the box from him. They had received their official photos long ago, but her colleague Jack, a photographer like Sofie, had made up his own album for them. He had declared it to be more quirky than traditional.

'Let me. I've been dying to see them!' she exclaimed as she tore at the wrapping paper, tossing it aside to lift the lid off the box. Peeling back tissue paper, she revealed a white leather-bound album.

Her photographer's eye told her Jack had done a fantastic job, but then she forgot all about composition and started to relive the day as each page was turned. It had been perfect, with blue skies and sunshine. Everyone had been happy, but none happier than herself and Lucas. Like all the men, he had been in full morning dress and just looking at him now turned her heart over.

They hadn't known each other very long—just a matter of a few short months—but they had known from the first that they were meant to be together. They had met whilst both were holidaying in Bali; however, there had only been time for a brief romance before she had to go home. What she hadn't known then was that Lucas was determined to see her again and had secretly arranged for her to take the official photos of the new London headquarters of the Antonetti Corporation. Lucas's father owned the company and Lucas was the managing director.

Not that she had been aware of that when she had gone there that first day. She had been so shocked to see him when she'd walked into the room that she had tripped on the corner of the carpet in his office and would have fallen to the floor had he not quickly gathered her into his arms. She had fallen in love at the same time. So deeply in love, she had known there was no cure. Especially when he'd swung her up into his arms with a grin that faded rapidly when he'd looked down at her.

'I didn't intend to say this now, but I can't wait any longer. I love you,' he had declared in a voice made thick by emotion.

'I love you too,' she had whispered back to him, so happy her heart had wings.

Then he had kissed her and, for Sofie, nothing had ever seemed so right. It wasn't a passionate kiss as kisses went, but it had rocked the world so that nothing could ever be the same again. Nor, she'd decided, when she had come back down to earth, would she ever want it to be. It had been an indescribable feeling, and she had felt it every time she looked at him from that moment on.

A whirlwind romance had led to a huge wedding—way beyond anything she had dreamed of—but they had wanted everyone to be there to share their happiness. Champagne had flowed, hundreds of photos had been taken and they had danced long into the night. The next day they had flown off to the Seychelles for four perfect weeks, before returning to the real world just a few weeks ago.

The photographs brought it all back, like the one of her dancing with her father. She remembered him telling her how beautiful she was, and it brought tears to her eyes now, as it had then. It had been the most wonderful of days.

'Ouch, there's my aunt with that awful hat!' Lucas declared with a wince and Sofie glanced over at the huge group picture he was looking at. It had been taken in the church grounds, which had, thankfully, been extensive. 'I don't remember inviting all these people, but we must have. Who's this? He isn't on my side, so he must be one of yours,' he asked her a moment later, and Sofie frowned.

'Where?' She tried to see who he meant in a sea of faces.

'Just there,' he said, pointing to the figure of a man standing at the end of one of the back rows.

Sofie looked where he was pointing and, the instant she did so, an icy hand grabbed at her heart. *No!* she cried out in silent despair. *Dear God, no!* She recognised who it was and all the joy went out of her as an arctic chill pierced her soul. How could he have been there? How could she not have sensed it?

'Don't know him?' Lucas prompted from beside her and she very nearly jumped because she had forgotten he was there, so caught up was she in the horror of the discovery.

Feeling the old shaking starting up inside her, Sofie gathered as much of her composure as she could in order to answer him and not make him aware that anything was wrong. 'No. No, I don't. He must be one of the boyfriends or husbands we never got to meet,' she responded reasonably, and was glad she sounded almost normal. She didn't feel it, though. The shaking was getting worse and she knew from experience that it would get the better of her soon. She didn't want Lucas to see that. Didn't want him to ask questions. She had enough of her own spinning around in her mind.

Glancing at the bedside clock, she gasped. 'My goodness, look at the time! We'll be late if we don't get a move on!' she added as she threw back the sheet. Scrambling from the bed, she snatched up the robe she had draped over a chair. 'You have that early meeting with…thingummy. You know who I mean. You'd better use the bathroom. I'll take a shower down the hall.'

She didn't give him time to argue the toss, but collected together some clothes and hurried out the door. Safe inside the bathroom in a spare bedroom, she shot the lock, dropped her clothes on the floor and sank back against the door, the shaking now a visible. Sofie pressed a hand over her mouth, but a whimper escaped all the same, and she sank down to the floor, dropping her head on her knees and wrapping her arms tightly around her waist.

Why now? she wanted to know. It had been some years since she had last seen that man. So many years that she had believed herself free of him, but that photograph proved how wrong she had been. Tears streamed down her cheeks as she rocked backwards and forwards. It made her feel physically sick to know that he had been there at the church. Waiting. Watching. Then he had joined on the end of a group photo, just as if he belonged there, knowing that she would see it and realise he was still around.

Her stomach heaved then and she scrambled to the toilet just in time. Afterwards she wiped her face with tissue and sank back weakly against the tiled wall. The shaking had stopped, thankfully, and probably wouldn't return now the first shock was over.

Her heart ached. She had dared to be happy. Had dared to look forward, not back. To what end? Nothing had changed. Gary Benson was still there. And to think she had once thought him sweet and kind!

She had been nineteen when they'd met, and they had been photography students at the same college. He had seemed normal enough, but before long she had discovered he wasn't. He was an ill man who was fixated on her. She had ended their relationship after only a few dates because he had smothered her with feelings she didn't share. He had been convinced she had to love him because he loved her, and so he wouldn't take no for an answer. He would ring her at all times of the day or night, or turned up at her house and simply stood outside, waiting until she was compelled to come out to tell him to go away.

She had thought he had finally got the message when he'd stopped ringing her, but instead he had started following her. Of course her family had called the police and obtained a restraining order, but that hadn't stopped him stalking her. Nothing had, because he'd vanished before he could be caught, only to turn up on another day in another place.

Life had been a nightmare for almost two years, and then it had stopped. She had never known why. Over time she had come to believe that he had given up on her and transferred his 'affections' to some other poor woman. She was just grateful that her life had returned to normal.

Except normal wasn't the normal it had once been. The experience had shredded her confidence. She could no longer trust any man, for fear that they would turn into another Gary Benson. She had become reserved and cautious, preferring to concentrate on her work, and it had been a very long time before she had been able to stop looking over her shoulder to check if 'he' was there.

Time had been the healer, and the appearance of Lucas in her life. With him she had finally dared to trust again. So much so that she had forgotten about Gary Benson completely—until that photograph had turned up. She knew now that whatever had kept him from her had been temporary. He hadn't forgotten her. He still thought of her as his.

The presumption angered her as never before. How dared he think he could do this to her again? She wouldn't allow it! She would tell the police. Even if they had been unable to stop him before, that didn't mean they would fail her this time. Yet Gary Benson had done nothing except appear in a photograph where he shouldn't have been. That could hardly be described as stalking.

What should she do? Instinct said she ought to tell Lucas, but he had so much on his mind at the moment, with the planned takeover of another company, that she didn't want to bother him. She could wait a few days. Just knowing Lucas was here gave her the confidence to do that. He was the exact opposite of Gary Benson—upright, honourable. He had never given her a moment's doubt, and she was slowly but surely coming to believe he never would.

Yes, that was what she would do. Nevertheless, it sent chills through her to know that Benson must be around, watching her. She knew he was probably biding his time. The photograph was a reminder. He would crawl out of the woodwork when he was ready, and come knocking on her door. However, this time she wasn't the defenceless young woman of before. She had a strong man to protect her now.

As she thought it, Lucas knocked on the bathroom door. 'Hey! Have you fallen asleep in there?'

Having jumped a mile, Sofie shot to her feet, hand pressed to her heart. 'I'm almost ready,' she lied, stripping off her robe and stepping into the shower. 'Put some toast on for me.' She didn't think she could force even a bite down, but she knew she had to behave as if everything was normal. Just for a little while, until the pressure was off Lucas.

After she had washed and dressed in record time, Sofie went down to the kitchen, where Lucas was sitting at the table eating a bowl of cereal. Her heart turned over, for he was so very precious to her.

Lucas looked up, frowning a little when he saw her standing watching him. 'What's up, *caro*?'

Smiling to hide her worries, she shook her head. 'Nothing. I was just thinking how much I love you,' she told him, and he immediately held out his hand invitingly.

'Come over here and tell me that.'

She went, allowing him to pull her down on to his lap. Combing her hand through his hair, she looked deeply into his eyes. 'I love you, Lucas. Nothing will ever stop me loving you.'

He smiled. 'I'm glad you feel that way, because it's how I feel, too. I couldn't imagine life without you now. I'd show you, if I didn't have that meeting in an hour.'

How Sofie wished they could simply go back to bed and shut out the world, but they couldn't. So she cocked her head flirtatiously and smiled back. 'Well, you can give me a little something on account, couldn't you?'

Laughing, he moved so that she was lying back with only his arm to support her. 'Oh, yes, I could most certainly do that,' he growled sexily and kissed her.

It was the kind of kiss that raised their temperatures to boiling point and took their breath away at the same time. When Lucas raised his head again, they were both left wanting more.

'Maybe that wasn't such a good idea. Remember where we were and we'll take it from there later,' he told her in a gruff voice, and Sofie hopped off his lap with a groan.

'It's going to be a long day.'

He grinned wolfishly and stood up. 'Yes, but keep your thoughts on the night,' he advised as he took his jacket off the back of the chair and slipped it on. 'I have to go, *caro*. Think of me toiling away at the mill whilst you're having fun snapping photos.'

She would. She always did. He was never far from her thoughts.

Sofie walked him to the door of their Hampstead home and waved him off in his car as she did most mornings. However, as she turned away to close the door, a movement across the road caught her eye and she looked back. Immediately her blood ran cold when she recognised the man standing in the shade of a tree. As she stood, transfixed, he started to walk across the road towards her. Though he was the very last person she wanted to talk to, she had to face him. Had to know why he had come back. Descending the steps, she walked to the gate and waited, arms folded defensively.

Gary Benson stopped on the other side. He was a nondescript man, who was already running to seed. 'Hello, Sofie,' he greeted her as if only days had passed, not years, and she looked at him coldly.

'What do you want, Gary?' she asked abruptly, but her coldness, as ever, went unheeded.

'You. Only you.'

She knew from before that anger got her nowhere, so she strove to remain calm. 'You can't have me. I'm spoken for, remember.' The broad hint made him laugh delightedly.

'You saw me in the photo. I hoped you would. You looked lovely in white.'

Sofie drew in an angry breath. 'You had no right to be there. It was a private wedding.'

Gary did as he always did and ignored what he didn't want to hear. 'How could you marry him? You belong to me! You love me!'

She shook her head, heart quailing as she heard the same old words. 'No, I don't. I love my husband, not you.'

'You think you do, but once he's gone you'll realise you made a mistake. Things will be better then. You'll see,' he informed her complacently.

To Sofie he was making no sense at all. 'He's not going anywhere. You're the one who's going to go away. Go away and stay away,' she commanded him, in as firm a voice as she could muster. Gary merely smiled.

'You know you don't mean that, Sofie.'

There was no getting through to him, and that made her want to scream with frustration. 'I do mean it and, if you don't stop bothering me, I shall call the police.'

He grinned, with the supreme confidence of the sick mind. 'They're useless. Besides, I haven't done anything. You know I'd never hurt you. I adore you. I just want us to be together.'

She laughed in his face. 'You can't be serious!' she derided and for perhaps the first time she really saw him angry.

'Don't laugh at me, Sofie. I don't like people laughing at me!' he berated her, then turned and stomped away, anger in every step.

Sofie watched him go down the road and around the corner. Her mind was seething. Somehow she had got through his thick skin and hurt him. Maybe that would be enough to make him stay away. A seed of hope started to germinate inside her. Maybe this time she had actually won. Smiling to herself, she ran up the steps and into the house, feeling more hopeful than she had been an hour ago.

That evening Sofie prepared one of Lucas's favourite meals, as this was to be their last evening together for at least a week. He had to go away on business and she wanted to make tonight special. Whilst the dinner was cooking in the oven, she slipped upstairs to take a long, relaxing bath, leaving her skin soft and delicately scented. Then she changed into cream lounging trousers and a silky vest top. Glancing at her wristwatch, she saw time was getting on and, humming to herself, she skipped down the stairs and went into the lounge to mix a pair of fancy cocktails.

Lucas arrived home some fifteen minutes later and, as soon as she heard his key in the door, her body began to tingle with anticipation. Picking up a glass in each hand, she walked out into the hall to greet him.

'Hi,' she said huskily and, setting the glasses down on the hall table, slipped into his arms before he had even set his briefcase down. Arms around his neck, she hugged him tightly, taking in the scent and feel of him so that she could remember this moment during the long days he would be away.

'Hi yourself,' Lucas replied with a laugh, dropping his briefcase and enfolding her in his strong arms. 'What brought this on?'

Sofie let her head fall back so that she could see him and laughed softly. 'I missed you, that's all,' she told him, pressing her lips to his neck and jaw in a series of tantalisingly brief kisses.

'I missed you, too, *caro*,' he told her, and moved his head just enough to capture her lips with his own.

There was no way Sofie could hold back when she knew they were about to be parted for the first time since they had married. She kissed him with all the depth of love she felt for him, igniting the passion that was never far from the surface. If Lucas was surprised, it didn't last long. Soon he was swept away, returning her kisses with the equally powerful love he felt for her.

When they drew back a short while later, neither had any interest in eating.

'I don't know about you, but I have no appetite for food right now,' Lucas growled sexily, and Sofie stroked her finger across his lips.

'I thought you'd be hungry. I have a casserole in the oven,' she teased, sending him a sultry look from beneath her lashes.

He grinned, but there was no mistaking the heat of passion in his eyes. 'I am hungry…for you. Let's go to bed,' he suggested and, taking her agreement for granted, swept her up in his arms.

'Let me turn the oven down. We can eat later,' she countered quickly, and he carried her through to the kitchen so she could turn down the heat, then back out and upstairs to their bedroom.

Once there, clothing was tossed aside carelessly in their eagerness. Desire mounted swiftly as, naked, they tumbled on to the bed and reached for each other. Knowing that tonight was going to have to last her until he got back gave a greater depth of passion to Sofie's every kiss and caress. She wanted to show him without words just how very much she loved him, and the result was scintillating. All their senses were heightened, so that the room echoed to their mingled gasps and sighs of pleasure.

Nothing else existed in the whole world other than the two of them as they rolled over, limbs tangling, glistening bodies gliding against each other. Hot breath mingled as increasingly erotic kisses were exchanged, driving their senses wild and tightening the coils of desire inside them. The conflagration was burning too hot and bright to last long. Driven by a powerful need, their bodies came together, fitting perfectly, moving as one towards the desired moment of release. It came in a white-hot explosion that made them both cry out as they hurtled into that realm of space known only to lovers.

Aeons later, their hearts began to slow their frantic beating and reality returned once more. Sofie turned into Lucas's arms, holding him close. This week was going to feel like for ever.

Suddenly heartsick, she snuggled up to him and closed her eyes. 'I wish you didn't have to go away,' she sighed, and he pressed a kiss to the top of her head.

'I'd rather stay here, too, but it's only a week. It will go in a flash. We'll have a whole lifetime together after that.'

His words comforted her like nothing else. 'Hmm, a whole lifetime…sounds good,' she murmured, yawning. A week was nothing. She was just being silly.

She hadn't intended to sleep, but their lovemaking and her busy day got the better of her. Before she knew it, she was fast asleep. A moment later, Lucas joined her.

For the next couple of days Sofie kept herself busy with work. The photographer she worked for was fully booked and consequently gave her plenty to do. She missed Lucas terribly and couldn't wait for his nightly telephone calls. The sound of his voice made her feel less lonely, even if it couldn't fill the gap in their bed at night.

When Wednesday came along, she cheered herself up by telling herself it was only a couple of days until Lucas returned home—a feeling that vanished when he rang that evening.

'Sorry, *caro,* but I'm going to have to stay a few days longer. Things aren't quite going to plan,' he told her, and her heart sank to her boots.

'Oh, Lucas, no!' she exclaimed, emotional tears welling behind her eyes.

'I know, I know,' he soothed. 'It can't be helped. I've worked too hard on this to let it fall apart now. You understand, don't you?'

Of course she did, but it didn't make her feel any better. 'Yes, I understand,' she replied glumly, then winced as a feminine squeal echoed down the line, followed by the distinct sound of giggling. 'What's going on?' she asked sharply, sitting up, frowning.

'Oh, that's just some guys fooling around. We're taking a break and I'm by the pool. Look, *amore,* I don't have much time. Just remember I love you and I'll be home as soon as I possibly can. OK?'

'OK, Lucas. Love you,' she responded, trying to sound cheerful, but her heart was heavy when she set the receiver back down. A few more days sounded like a jail sentence. Not that there was anything she could do about it. She just had to get through it.

She slept badly that night and was consequently late getting up. Because she had a photo session at a client's house, she picked up the mail as she was leaving the house and stuffed it in her bag. She only discovered it later in the day, when she bought a sandwich for lunch and took it to a nearby park to eat it in peace.

Examining the small collection of envelopes, she recognised the usual bills and junk mail, but there was a large brown envelope at the bottom which had nothing but her name and address typed on it. Curious, she tore it open and reached inside for the contents. They were face down, but it was clear from the markings that what she held were photographs. Wondering who could be sending them to her, and thinking it might be more wedding photos a relative had decided to pass on, she turned them over.

A Post-it note was stuck to the front, with a brief message:

Do you know what your husband gets up to while he's away? Take a look at these.

Her stomach fell away, leaving her feeling as if she were poised at the edge of a precipice. Trembling fingers pulled the note away, revealing the top photograph, and she gasped as shock hit her like a sledgehammer. There was Lucas, with his arms around a woman she had never seen before. They were laughing and gazing into each other's eyes as if…

'No!' The cry left her lips though Sofie was unaware of saying anything. She flipped the photo up, revealing the next, and her heart cried out in pain, for this time they were kissing.

Shaking her head as if to deny what she was seeing, Sofie looked at each in turn, and in every one it was the same woman, even if the background was different. Anyone could see that the couple were obviously in the midst of a passionate affair. She closed her eyes, trying not to see them, but her brain just replayed each one over and over.

Feeling sick, she forced herself to keep calm. It couldn't be true. Lucas couldn't be having an affair! Yet she had the evidence in her hands. But where had they come from? Who had sent them? She searched the envelope, but there was nothing inside, only the stark note. Someone had wanted her to know the truth, but wished to remain anonymous.

It left a nasty taste in her mouth. That person need not be a friend, which gave Sofie a moment's pause. Despite what she saw, was it true? Could there be some other plausible explanation? That fragile framework of trust she had built since meeting Lucas made her want to believe there was an answer, and the only way to know was to ask him.

Lucas wouldn't lie to her. She trusted him, and trust was everything. Reaching into her bag for her mobile phone, she flipped it open and groaned when she realised she had forgotten to charge it. There had to be a phone box nearby, so she shoved everything piecemeal into her bag and hurried off to find one. When she did, it was occupied, and she had to wait a nerve-racking ten minutes before she could step inside and close the door.

She didn't care that it would be the middle of the night where Lucas was, but dialled the number of the hotel he was staying at. There was a long wait whilst the call was put through to his room, but finally it was answered. She was taking in a deep breath when a voice spoke.

'Hello? This had better be important.' A distinctly feminine disgruntled voice echoed in Sofie's ear.

Her heart stopped, and she frowned. 'Sorry. They were supposed to be putting me through to Lucas Antonetti's room. There must have been a mistake,' she began to apologise.

'There's no mistake, honey. This is Lucas's room. Just you hold on and I'll get him for you.' Stunned, Sofie could only listen to the noises at the other end of the line. 'Hey, Lucas, you gorgeous hunk of man. Get out of bed. There's a phone call for you!'

Sofie gasped in disbelief as her whole world began to shatter around her. She didn't need to wait to hear more, but slammed down the receiver and tumbled out of the phone box in a state of near devastation. The only thoughts going around her mind were that the photos hadn't lied. It was all true. All most horribly true!

Looking around her, everything felt alien and she just wanted to get away. Go home and wait for the pain to go away. She flagged down a passing taxi and sank into the seat, dropping her head in her hands. How could Lucas do this to her? She had trusted him! It had taken every ounce of courage she had possessed to trust him and put her faith in their future together, and now it was gone. Shattered into a million irretrievable pieces.

Dear God, it was Gary Benson all over again. He had

turned her life into a nightmare, and now Lucas had betrayed her. She couldn't take it again. She just couldn't take it!

That same thought was in her mind when she got home. Only it didn't feel like home any more. It was a place of deception and treachery and she couldn't spend another night in it. As she looked round the lounge she had spent so many happy hours in, she knew that she was going to leave Lucas. However much she loved him, the trust was gone. If she stayed, she would never trust a thing he said or did, and that would destroy her, so she had to go.

Not just go, but vanish completely, so that she would never see him again. It was the only way, for her love for him might undermine her resolve if she saw him. It might tempt her to stay and try to live with the doubts. No, she must go and never look back. The prospect almost made her break down, but she knew she had to be strong. Later she could fall apart. When it was done. When it was all over.

It was that strength of purpose which made it possible for her to pick up the phone and call her parents. She couldn't leave without explaining why. After a few rings, her mother answered.

'Hi, Mum. I…I just wanted to tell you not to be worried if you don't hear from me for a while,' she said, her voice catching as she worked hard to keep her emotions under control.

Her mother instantly sensed there was something wrong. 'Why? What is it, Sofie? What's happened?'

Sofie drew in a shaky breath. 'I'm leaving Lucas, Mum,' she declared tautly, and heard her mother gasp.

'Leaving Lucas? But why? What's gone wrong? I thought you were so happy.' Her mother sounded almost as distraught as Sofie felt.

'I can't explain now. Just know that I have to do this. I

can't…' Her voice broke and she had to bite her lip hard. 'I don't know when I'll see you again, but I'll write to you.'

'Oh, Sofie, don't do anything hasty. Come and talk to us. Perhaps we can help.'

Sofie blinked back scalding tears. 'Nobody can help. I'm sorry, Mum. I love you both. Don't worry about me. Goodbye,' she ended on a broken whisper and set the phone down before her mother could say anything else.

Almost immediately the phone started ringing again, but she ignored it. Going up to the bedroom, she took two large cases from the dressing room and packed everything that she intended to take with her. She hefted them downstairs, leaving them in the hall whilst she went to the desk in the lounge and wrote the hardest letter she had ever had to write. She simply told Lucas she was leaving and that he shouldn't waste his time looking for her. She wasn't coming back. Then she sealed it in an envelope, wrote his name on the outside and propped it up against the clock on the mantelpiece.

Finally she rang for a taxi and, whilst the driver stowed her cases, she locked the front door and dropped the keys back through the letterbox. As she went down the steps for the last time, she walked away from all her hopes and dreams.

'Do you know which station has trains going north?' she asked the driver.

'Depends which part of the north you want, love,' he told her and she shrugged.

'Just take me to the closest one,' she told him and sat back, closing her eyes.

It was over. She had done what she had to do. Now she had to find a way to live the rest of her life without Lucas.

CHAPTER ONE

'WELL, I'm glad I don't have to tell him that!' Sofie exclaimed with a laugh as she turned to gather a fresh glass of champagne from the tray of a passing waiter.

Everything was running smoothly, just as she had planned. When her boss had put forward the idea of a photographic competition, she had agreed enthusiastically, never expecting to have the job of arranging and running it. However, it had been a challenge, and she was always prepared to stretch herself. That she would also have to host the award ceremony and help give out the prizes was not what she'd wanted. Drawing attention to herself was still something she preferred not to do. Staying out of the limelight was vital. However, as this was only a local competition, with no chance of a report getting into anything other than local newspapers, she had felt safe in agreeing to do it.

Life had been far from easy these past few years. She had scrimped and saved, trying to keep her head above water by doing any job that turned up. In the end, though, circumstances had forced her to apply for assistance under a new name, and life had improved gradually. Now she had a steady job and a small rented cottage to live in. Even though she had never seen anyone from her past life, it was hard to make herself stop looking over her shoulder all the time. She had come almost as far north as it was possible to go and still be in the same country. Paying cash for everything, she had left no paper trail behind her. Sofie Antonetti had vanished off the face of the earth that day six years ago, and in her place was Sofie Talbot, photographer's assistant, who kept herself very much to herself. If she was lonely, she never let on. If she was sad, only her pillow knew.

With a satisfied sigh she ran her eye around the room, checking that nothing had gone awry. The action took her away from the group she was chatting to and brought the doorway of the room into her line of sight—just in time to see the tall figure of a man walk in and pause to survey his surroundings. Shock tore through her with all the destructive force of an earthquake, because this was not just any man. She recognised him instantly. Would know him if a hundred years had passed, for he was locked in her heart and would always remain there.

It was Lucas. He had found her.

She couldn't move in those first few seconds, not even a muscle. This was the day she had dreaded for so long, and yet had longed for in the very depths of her soul. To see him again filled her with unbridled joy, as she had come to think she never would look upon his beloved face again. Oh, she had daydreamed about walking into him in a crowd, or sheltering from a summer storm under a tree and finding him doing the same, but without any real hope of it happening. Yet now it had.

The first shock was passing and pent-up emotion rose to choke her throat and bring the smart of tears to her eyes. He hadn't seen her yet and she took advantage of it.

Through a crystal blur, she ate him up like a woman who

had wandered hungrily in a wasteland and had suddenly found food. She had loved this man beyond reason and doubt from the first moment they had met. There had always been a certain something about him which had made her senses leap in a way quite out of the ordinary for her. No other man had been able to hold a candle to what she had experienced with Lucas. This awareness had hit her like the proverbial ton of bricks. All her senses had come to attention, and she had been so attuned to him it had been uncanny. So much so that, whenever he had entered the same room as herself, she had felt it immediately. Like electricity charging up the air.

She could feel it now, as she stared at him. He hadn't changed. His hair was the same blue-black she remembered, though he must be thirty-six now. In one of the Italian designer suits he had always preferred, a glass of champagne in one hand and the other casually slipped into his trouser pocket, he was the epitome of a man in control of himself and the world he lived in. It was an air of *savoir-faire* which she had always found immensely attractive.

Was there any surprise then that she had fallen headlong in love with him and married him, all in a whirlwind matter of months? She would do it again in an instant—except for one huge problem. Whilst she still loved him, and always would, she knew in her heart that he could no longer love her.

That thought brought her back to the reality of the present, and the fact that she was standing staring at a man who would never be as pleased to see her as she was to see him. It galvanised her into action and she turned away hastily, hoping he hadn't seen her. What had she been thinking of, staring at him so longingly? This wasn't a happy ending, rather the start of what could turn out to be another nightmare.

Of course, that thought turned her stomach over and she

sipped at her champagne as a much needed bolster to her nerve. Think, she ordered herself. Be logical. Because she was hiding from him, that didn't mean he had found her. This could all be pure coincidence. Why would he look for her here, of all places? She wasn't even using the name he knew her by. Wasn't it more likely that he had business in the area? He could even be staying in this very hotel and had looked in at the function out of pure curiosity.

That had to be it, she decided on a wobbly sigh. Not that it helped her very much if he didn't leave in the next half hour. If he were still here at nine, then there was no way he could be prevented from seeing her. Nine o'clock was the designated time for the presentation of awards to the winners of the photography competition, a task she had been looking forward to.

Photography was her joy and getting back into it, even in such a small way, had gone a long way to giving her a sense of purpose. Life had started to have meaning again, not just days to be got through without the love and support of the man she loved. She had been happy. However, that happiness could be in danger if Lucas didn't leave soon. If he saw her, there would be the inevitable confrontation, and Sofie feared that the most, because even though she had left Lucas with good reason she knew he would have been furious that she had just disappeared, and there were things she had never told him, the biggest of which would condemn her in his eyes for ever.

With nowhere to hide, all Sofie could do for the moment was leave the room and lose herself in the crowds swelling the other reception rooms. Soon she was caught up in the laughing, chatting groups and was able to breathe a little more easily. Leastways she did until she felt a subtle change in the air and knew that Lucas had entered the room. She tensed immediately and prayed he would move on—but then the back of her neck started to prickle and she knew those endlessly fascinating blue eyes were upon her.

She turned slowly, compelled by a force too strong to deny, her heart thumping sickeningly in her chest. She felt as if she were moving in slow motion, and indeed the noise around her faded into a drone as she saw Lucas standing at the back of the room, eyes fixed on her intently. A sense of inevitability sank over her and her eyelashes slowly fluttered down then up again.

Sofie must have stopped breathing, though she was unaware of it, for now she drew in a long ragged breath. After so long, to finally meet his eyes again was stunning and the connection shot across the room between them like a shaft of lightning. She couldn't see his expression; she only knew the experience was as powerful as it had ever been.

She waited for him to come towards her, but he didn't, and confusion set in. As if he sensed it, a faint smile curved his lips and Sofie hurriedly turned away, brain desperately searching for a reason for his actions. Why hadn't he come and spoken to her? It was what she had expected. Then, of course, she understood. He was biding his time. If and when they talked, it would be on his terms. It was a subtle reminder of the circumstances of her leaving him. That had been under her control, this was to be under his.

A fact she soon confirmed by slowly making her way through one room and then another. Even though her sensitive radar could sense when he followed, she glanced over her shoulder to check. It was clear. When she moved, he moved, but always maintained the same distance between them. He was playing cat and mouse with her, and she was no cartoon character who could turn the tables on him. All she knew was that she couldn't allow him to see just how anxious he was making her.

'There you are! I lost you for a moment.'

Sofie spun round, a slightly guilty smile springing to her lips at the sight of David Lacey, her boss and the instigator of the evening. She had forgotten all about him the instant she'd laid eyes on Lucas. 'I...er...just came in here to get a fresh drink,' she lied uncomfortably, waggling her glass at him.

'That's funny, I thought I was doing that,' David remarked, holding up two glasses, but Sofie wasn't listening to him, her eyes had automatically started to search for Lucas again. She found him not too far away, watching the pair of them intently. 'And the dog ran away with the ham bone,' David ended dryly, which was where she tuned in again.

Her nerves jumping like fleas, she half-turned away from Lucas and beamed up at her boss. 'Hmm? I'm sorry, what did you say?'

Not surprisingly, David frowned. 'Forget it, it wasn't important. Are you all right, Sofie?' he asked in concern, then glanced at her glass. 'How many of those have you had?' He set the spare glass he had brought with him on a passing tray.

Sofie took a steadying breath, telling herself to get a grip. The last thing she needed was for David to ask awkward questions. 'Sorry. It's speech time soon and I'm a tad distracted.' Hell's bells, what an understatement that was, and so far from the truth! Knowing that Lucas was watching her every move was hardly conducive to calm. 'Don't worry, this is only my second glass.' She never drank much and had abandoned the first glass because it had become warm and lost its fizz.

'I see everybody who is anybody has turned out for this shindig,' David remarked, glancing round the room. 'Everywhere I look there's a familiar face. Although having said that, there is one person I don't know. Have you any idea who the man in the suit by the door is?'

Sofie's heart gave a wild kick, for she could guess who he meant. 'What man?' she asked gruffly, wondering what to do, because if she pleaded ignorance and then Lucas decided to come over, she would be caught out in a lie.

'It doesn't matter. He's gone,' David replied, not realising how that would affect her.

Sofie turned, her eyes flying to the spot where she had last seen Lucas, and her spirits sank like a stone when she discovered he had moved away. As much as she had dreaded having a confrontation with him, her worst fear was that he would go and she would never see him again!

With something approaching anxiety her eyes scanned the room, searching for him and failed. Completely distraught, she couldn't believe he had gone without making contact, when he had spent the whole evening watching her. Disappointment weighed heavily on her and she couldn't explain why. She knew the best thing was for him to go. They couldn't go back, and had no future. Let him be gone, the logical part of her brain told her. Let this be the end of it. Sadly, her shattered heart would always crave more.

Which was why, uncharacteristically, she took a large gulp of champagne and almost emptied the glass. Seeing it, David's brows rose and he plucked the glass from her fingers.

'Steady on! You'll get tipsy doing that on an empty stomach. Wait here. I'll go get us something to eat,' he decided, setting their glasses aside, and would have gone off in search of the buffet had she not placed a staying hand on his arm.

'No, don't. I'm fine, really,' she lied bravely, as her nerves were a mess and she was as far from fine as it was possible to get. 'It's almost time for my speech anyway.'

It was a relief when she had to go up and help present the awards. Making small talk with David as if nothing was the matter had been excruciatingly difficult. The last thing she felt like doing was smiling for the cameras, but it was all part of the job and she formed her lips into as near normal a smile as possible.

Casually glancing around the sea of faces below them, her heart leapt when her eyes found Lucas once more. So he hadn't gone! As if he knew exactly what she had been thinking, he raised his glass in silent salute and her thoughts scattered to the four winds as she realised nothing was over yet.

Unfortunately she lost sight of him again when she and the winners descended to the floor and were surrounded by admiring friends and family. It took time extricating herself from everyone who wanted to speak to her, but as soon as she was alone Sofie searched the room again, with the same negative result as earlier. Tired of playing games that had her emotions see-sawing wildly, and knowing she wasn't in the right frame of mind to make small talk with anyone right then, she sought for a means of escape and found it beyond the door to the terrace.

Outside in the warm summer night air, she made her way to the parapet and leaned on it, looking out over the city. The light was fading and all around the city began to twinkle. She had never regretted moving north, only the circumstances that had made it necessary. She had done a good job of vanishing off the map and couldn't have chosen a better place to make a fresh start, even though she had been terrified that Lucas would find her.

When time passed and he hadn't discovered her hiding place, she had started to think she was safe, and look what had happened—Lucas had come back into her life. The very thing she had been afraid of for so long, because, however much her heart wanted to see him, her brain knew it wasn't safe to do so. Now, more than ever. It had gone beyond the reason for her leaving. There were things he didn't know and, though he had a right to know them, she feared what he would do if he found out.

Life, she had learned years ago, could be cruel, causing people to make choices they shouldn't have to make. It had broken her heart then and she had barely survived. She didn't think she would be so lucky if fate played its hand a second time.

Just then a soft breeze blew her shoulder-length brown hair across her face and at the same time a tingle of awareness ran down her spine. She spun round, her breath hitching in her throat as she saw the source of her turmoil stroll out of the nearby shadows.

Up close he was still the handsomest man she had ever seen. A shaft of light from the windows highlighted the almost blue-black of his hair and the intense blue of his eyes. She could remember those eyes smiling at her with such love in them it had taken her breath away. Now, though, it was hard to read what he was thinking. He had closed himself off from her.

Lucas stopped a few feet away, a faintly mocking smile hovering around the corners of his mouth, whilst his eyes ranged over her. Once upon a time such a glance would have sent delicious tingles along her nerve-endings as they passed, but there was no warmth in his eyes surveying of her now. It left her feeling bereft, a faint hope dying before she was even aware of its existence. She was inordinately glad when he finally held her gaze.

'What took you so long?' he said huskily, the rich tone of his voice delighting her senses as it always had. However, the question made her jump.

'L-long? I...er...' she had to cough to clear a dry throat. 'I don't understand,' she returned in genuine confusion, her emotions making it hard for her brain to work. Facing the man she loved six years after walking out on him was not a situation she had ever planned for. Quite the opposite.

Lucas shook his head disappointedly. 'Of course you do. You've been watching me all evening, and I've enjoyed watching you watch me. That's why I knew when you couldn't see me you'd come in search of me.'

Sofie caught her breath, her pulse racing anxiously with her inner turmoil. 'That wasn't the reason. It was hot and I needed… That is…' Realising she was almost babbling, she closed her eyes and drew in some steadying air. 'I thought you were gone.'

'Hoped, you mean,' Lucas returned silkily, and she licked her lips nervously to moisten them.

'Yes…no…w-whatever!' she responded jerkily, then made an effort to get a grip. 'Why would I want to see you? We have nothing to say to each other,' she told him more firmly, because denial was all the defence she had. She needed him to walk away from her, for should he find out about her sin, he would never forgive her. In his place, neither would she.

'On the contrary, I think you and I have one hell of a lot to say to one another, Mrs Antonetti!' he shot back, and there was no doubting the underlying edge of anger in the coldness of his tone.

Sofie flinched, knowing he had a right to be angry. More than he knew. 'Lucas…' she responded helplessly, and something wild flashed in his eyes.

'Ah, Lucas! Do you know that the sound of my name on your lips once used to send me up in flames?' he challenged sarcastically and, because she did remember, it drove a knife into her heart.

'Please…' she breathed achingly, knowing she had enraged

him by leaving the way she had. She should have stayed and confronted him with the proof of his treachery, but it hardly mattered now. That he had betrayed her was irrelevant, and her fears that he would have lied his way out of it and somehow convinced her to stay. She was playing for higher stakes, and the cost of losing didn't bear thinking about.

Lucas stepped closer, eyes glittering. 'You used to say that, too, when you begged me to make love to you. Do you remember that, Sofie? Do you remember any of it?'

Dear Lord, she remembered everything. Nothing was forgotten. None of the happiness, none of the heartache. However much she might want to throw his words back in his face, she had to be careful. She had too much to lose now.

'Th-there's no point in remembering. I put the past behind me.' It was a lie. Not a day went by when she didn't remember and long for what was lost.

A sneer curved the lips she had once craved to kiss. 'How convenient. The trouble is, the past has a habit of rearing up and biting you when you least expect it. As it did with me, when I walked into the hotel yesterday and saw your picture advertising this event.'

Her nerves jolted as she heard that. 'Then you weren't...' She cut the question off, aware of what it would reveal, but Lucas was far too astute to miss it.

'Weren't looking for you? No, I'm here on business, so you can imagine my shock. My errant wife, whom I had sought from one end of the country to the other, was hiding in plain sight,' Lucas explained with a mocking laugh.

Her chin came up. 'I wasn't hiding,' she denied, and it had been true once. She *hadn't* started out hiding from Lucas, she just hadn't wanted to see him again, knowing that her love for him made her weak. However, circumstances had changed, and she had ended up hiding from him for totally different reasons.

One eyebrow lifted in a gesture she remembered so well it tweaked her heartstrings. 'Then why the change of name, if not because you didn't want me to find you?'

Sofie's stomach lurched anxiously. She had never found it easy to lie but, with things the way they were, she had to find some way to make him go away and leave her alone. 'Because... Because...' Invention failed her. Oh, God, what could she say? Her mind flailed around seeking inspiration and locked on to the first it could find. 'I was th-thinking of, um...opening my own studio,' she told him, her hands gesturing uneasily. 'At one time,' she added, hoping he would accept that, but the scoffing look he sent her spoke of her failure.

'I might have believed it had your name been Smith or Brown, but my name sounds professional to me. So tell me, *amore,* why didn't you call yourself Sofie Antonetti? You were entitled to, as my wife.'

'Stop calling me that!' she snapped, nerves so ragged she could scream.

Her response brought a sardonic curl to his lips. 'Why? It's who you are,' he told her mockingly. 'Sofie Antonetti, my wife.'

Her lips parted on a faint gasp, whilst shock slammed her again. Surely he couldn't mean... 'But... I told you not to try and find me, to forget me. I thought...'

Lucas tipped his head on one side. 'That I would divorce you. Think again, Mrs Antonetti. There was no way on this earth that I was going to walk away from you without an explanation. So, that begs the question, why didn't you divorce me? Now, what could be the reason for that? Ah, yes, because if you did I would find out where you were, and you didn't want that, did you?' he finished curtly.

Sofie swallowed hard. 'I deserted you. Right was on your side,' she pointed out huskily.

A dark look entered his eyes. 'You're darn right it was. You said you loved me. Couldn't wait to marry me. Then, a few months after the wedding, you vanish into thin air. Did you honestly think I would put that all down to experience and forget you? Dream on, Sofie.'

She should have known that a man who felt as strongly as Lucas wouldn't let anything go. He didn't know she knew about his liaison. All he knew was that she had left him and she couldn't put him right. Not now. Not ever. 'I'm sorry. I made a mistake.'

His laugh was hollow. 'You certainly did. Walking out on me was the wrong thing to do. You owe me, Sofie, and, now that I've found you, I fully intend to collect.'

Sofie stared at him, knowing that this was one of the reasons she had hidden herself away. She had always known he was a passionate man and that his anger would be just as tempestuous as the love he'd claimed to feel for her. Maybe he had loved her, but it hadn't stopped him having an affair. Yet, however much he wanted answers, there were none she could give him, as she dared not let him guess her secret for fear of what he might do.

So she had to hold back her emotions and be as firm in her resolve as she had been when she'd left him. 'There's nothing to collect. If I hurt you, I'm sorry, but what I did was for the best. I'll say it again. Forget you ever met me, Lucas. We were never meant to be together. Have your meeting and go home. Please.'

Lucas laughed at her. 'Just because you were once able to get me to do anything you asked, don't imagine you still can. I shall stay here until *all* my business is settled.'

It wasn't what she wanted to hear and it set her nerves twitching again. 'Fine. Stay, but don't bother me. You're not wanted, Lucas,' she told him bluntly, thinking there was nothing else she could do.

Blue eyes narrowed on her. 'Why? Because you've replaced me? Was that him, the man I saw you with? What did you do with him? Send him off on an errand and then abandon him?'

It was close enough to the truth to be uncomfortable, because she hadn't given him a thought since coming out here. 'David's used to me. He won't mind.' At least she hoped he wouldn't.

One eyebrow quirked. 'Poor man, to be dismissed so casually. Perhaps I ought to tell him he's dating a married woman.'

Not wanting him to speak to anyone about her, Sofie had to set the record straight. 'You don't have to worry about David, he's my boss,' she corrected hastily.

'That had better be true, *amore*. I wouldn't want you to end this first meeting on a lie,' he advised her softly, staring down into her widened eyes.

'First and last meeting,' she corrected firmly, standing her ground, though her legs were beginning to wobble badly.

'This isn't over. You *will* be seeing me again. Now, much as I would prefer to stay and continue this fascinating conversation with you, I have a telephone conference to take,' he informed her, stepping back as he did so.

Sofie straightened up, her heart suddenly racing again. 'Please stay away from me, Lucas!' she called after him as he moved off.

'Can't be done, I'm afraid. Not now I've finally found you again,' he refused coldly, and was gone before she could utter another word.

The strength went out of her legs the instant he passed from view and Sofie sank back against the wall with a shaky sigh. This couldn't be happening! After all she had been through, how could life turn on her this way? Because the fates had decided to give Lucas a throw of the dice. The scales had to be balanced. Only the fates didn't know that there was more at stake than her having to explain her actions six years ago. Now she had even more to lose, and the possibility was absolutely terrifying.

'You're getting to be harder to keep track of than my three-year-old niece!' David declared from directly in front of her, making her jump because she hadn't noticed his approach.

Guilt washed over her for having abandoned him twice tonight, and she pulled herself together in a hurry. 'I'm sorry, David. I popped outside for some air.'

'So I saw,' he said dryly, bringing faint colour to her cheeks. 'That was the man in the suit I saw earlier. Who is he?'

Sofie knew that if she denied all knowledge she would only look foolish later if the lie was discovered, so she told the truth—so far as it went. 'His name is Lucas Antonetti. He's here on business,' she revealed, knowing David could find that much out by asking at the desk.

He frowned. 'Antonetti? Now, why does that name ring a bell, I wonder?'

Sofie's stomach gave an unwelcome jolt, as she hadn't considered David would have heard of Lucas. 'Perhaps he's been in the papers,' she proffered, hoping to end further speculation.

'Probably,' David agreed easily. 'Anyway, when are you going to see him again?'

She couldn't help tensing at the simple question. 'I'm not,' she denied instantly, much to David's surprise. 'What made you ask such a silly question?' she added, with a nervous laugh that fooled neither of them.

'Because I saw him watching you whilst you were on the stage, and if ever a man was interested in a woman, he was.'

Sofie had to stifle the urge to laugh wildly. 'You're mistaken.'

Deaf to the less than subtle hint, David shook his head. 'I think not. He couldn't take his eyes off you!'

That was about as much as Sofie could take, and she straightened, glad to feel her legs were now supporting her. 'We were simply talking. I have absolutely no intention of meeting him again!' she insisted sharply and David blinked in surprise.

'Sorry. I just thought… Well, never mind. I'll shut up now,' he apologised, the words tumbling all over themselves, leaving Sofie feeling wretched.

'I'm sorry for jumping down your throat like that,' she apologised, too, feeling tiredness wash over her. 'Would you mind if I went home now, David? I'm exhausted.'

'Of course, Sofie. You poor thing, you look totally drained,' he declared in some concern. 'You made everything look so easy, I didn't realise how tired you must be. You did a grand job tonight and I'm proud of you,' he added as he took her arm through his to escort her out.

At that time of night it wasn't a long journey from the hotel to her cottage. David saw her to the door, then left with a friendly wave. Letting herself in, Sofie closed the door gently behind her. She paused momentarily, looking up the stairs, then walked into the sitting room where a young woman glanced up from the book she was reading and smiled.

'Hi, Annie, is everything OK?' Sofie enquired, watching the woman gather up her things, getting ready to leave.

'Not a peep all evening,' Annie reported, taking the money Sofie offered her. 'Just give us a bell when you need us again.'

'I will. Thank you, Annie,' Sofie promised, seeing the girl

out and watching whilst she walked to the next cottage and opened the front door. Then Sofie climbed the stairs and went to a door which stood slightly ajar.

Pushing it open carefully, she slipped inside and walked over to the bed, looking down at the small figure sleeping there. Her heart tightened painfully, because her dark-haired little angel was the spitting image of his father—Lucas. This was the secret she so feared would be discovered. If Lucas was bent on revenge for the way she had walked out on him, what would he do if he ever discovered she had withheld the knowledge that he had a son?

Now her heart quailed, for the possibilities were terrifying, and her hand was trembling as she ran it gently over Tom's hair. He sighed heavily and she waited until she was sure he was still asleep before kissing his forehead and silently leaving the room again. Outside she steadied herself with a hand on the wall. What was she going to do? Lucas had betrayed her, so why should she be the one to suffer more? He was the one in the wrong, and she had been justified in leaving him. Why should there be more?

The answer was painfully obvious. Because two wrongs didn't make a right. Because everything had to be paid for sooner or later and, for her sin of omission, that time was now.

CHAPTER TWO

WITH a soft moan of distress, Sofie crossed to her bedroom, switching on the light but leaving the door ajar so she could hear Tom if he woke in the night. Kicking off her shoes, she walked over to the window, rubbing her palms up and down her arms as if chilled, though she knew that sensation came from within.

Was Lucas standing at his window too, staring out, wondering if she was thinking of him? No, he was too confident for that. He *knew* she was thinking of him, worrying what he was going to do. Now that he had found her, by accident though it might have been, he wasn't about to walk away until he had answers. She couldn't blame him, but oh, how she wished things could have been different.

Their relationship had started out with such passion and excitement, joy and hope for the future. Even now she smiled when she pictured him looking down at her with love in his eyes. Her heart ached with the memory and the knowledge that, by her later actions, she had forfeited the right ever to see such a look again.

Yet would she believe a declaration of love, even if he were inclined to give it? Her heart would, because she still loved him so desperately, but her head knew he had lied to her. He had broken her trust, and that could never be put right. She would never have believed he could do what he had, but she had the proof. She wouldn't believe him. Could not.

Sofie sighed heavily, the weight of her sense of betrayal hard to bear now that she had seen Lucas again. Her eye was drawn to the jewellery box which sat on her dressing table and she went to it, taking out the top layer and removing what lay hidden there. Tears glistened in her eyes as she stared at the diamond encrusted wedding band she held in her right hand, so that when she looked at the photograph in her left hand it was almost a blur.

Blinking hard, she went back to the window and sat down on the tiny window seat. Biting her lip, she stared at the two figures in the picture. It was the only one she had taken with her when she'd left. It was of herself and Lucas, on their wedding day, and looking so happy it hurt. Of course, that was because she hadn't known that, for all his charm and passion, he was fickle. Love obviously meant something else to him.

Even knowing of his betrayal, leaving Lucas had been so painful she had cried herself to sleep more nights than she could count. There had seemed to be no end to the tears. She couldn't help wondering where he was, what he was doing. The longing to hear his voice had urged her to reach for the telephone more than once, but reason had always made her draw back at the last minute. She had fallen under his spell once, with the result that he had broken her heart. She couldn't risk falling under it again.

More like an automaton than a human being, she had got through each day as best she could. It had been like walking through a dark, endless tunnel, with no light at the end of it. Until she had discovered she was pregnant. That day she had started to live again. Life had purpose once more, now that she had a precious baby to take care of.

Of course, once the initial euphoria had worn off, she had realised she was in an untenable position. The baby wasn't just hers, and the knowledge tore her in two. She knew it was only right and fair that Lucas should know he had a child but, after what he had done, she could not contact him. Though it left her with a heavy burden of guilt, she was too hurt to change her mind, and she would just have to live with the consequences.

It hadn't been easy, living her life without the man she loved, but Tom's arrival had helped her. Loving him had been the easiest thing to do, and concentrating on him had kept her from despairing about how different her life might have been, had Lucas not proven to have feet of clay. Having made the hard decisions, she had done her best to put the past behind her and get on with her life.

Unfortunately, her past had just caught up with her.

Fear rushed through her as she realised how vulnerable she was. What was she going to do about Tom? Having kept him secret from Lucas, how could she reveal his existence now? Lucas would never forgive her, and that would be his right, but what might he do? Her heart knew that he would want his son, and yet she couldn't lose Tom. After all that had happened, that would be too much to bear!

Tears burnt her eyes and she pressed her hand over trembling lips. In her mind she could hear her grandmother's gentle voice uttering one of her truisms: *be sure your sins will find you out.* Oh, God, she knew she had sinned, but what else could she have done? She couldn't have returned to Lucas, as that would have meant living in a state of constant doubt. Waiting for him to betray her again. Break her heart again. Because he surely would have. He had proved he was capable of it. What love he had felt for her hadn't stopped him, and her leaving him must have destroyed even that. So she had stayed away, thinking he would forget her and get on with his life.

Only now she was discovering Lucas had other ideas. He hadn't divorced her, nor forgotten her. He wanted answers. He wanted payment for what she had done to him.

A single tear snaked its way down her cheek. Of course he did. Never mind the double standard. He was a man whose pride had been wounded by his wife leaving him. He wanted revenge. Wanted to confront her. Unfortunately she wasn't prepared, never could have been, for a confrontation with her husband. Yet one was upon her now, and she had to be strong. However wrong it was, she had to keep Tom a secret still. All she had to get through was one more meeting and then Lucas would be gone and her life could return to normal.

A strangled laugh escaped her. She hardly knew what normal was any more. It was so hard to lie, yet that was all she had to protect herself. When Lucas turned up, as she was certain he would, she must tell him what he wanted to hear. Tell him anything that would make him walk away—this time for ever.

Pain seared through her at the thought, and she leant her head back against the wall, drawing in a ragged breath. The severity of that pain told her a truth she had avoided—that deep in her heart she had always hoped that one day he would come back into her life, tell her he loved her and forgave her, and everything would be all right again. It was the vain hope of a lost and lonely, broken-hearted woman.

Sofie hugged herself as silent tears flowed. Nothing had changed. There was to be no happy ever after for them, because she could never trust him again. His betrayal had destroyed forever the fragile hope she had that there was one man out there she could put her faith in. She might long for a fairy godmother to wave her wand and make everything right, but she knew she lived in the real world. Even if he wanted her back, she would be afraid to trust him, because that would make her vulnerable again. Love without trust was an empty shell.

The following few days were a nightmare roller coaster of highs and lows. One moment confident she could get through meeting Lucas again with her secret intact, the next despairing, for she knew how hard it was going to be. How could she hide a five-year-old boy, who was used to running in and out of the house at will? She had hardly slept the last three nights, anticipating Lucas's arrival at any moment, but so far he had failed to appear.

She didn't think for a minute that he had given up the idea of seeing her again and gone home. He was either very busy with what had brought him north in the first place, or intent on making her squirm. Probably both, she thought with an atavistic shiver.

Now it was Monday and she had dropped Tom off at school on her way in to work. He had been in a grumpy mood all weekend and she guessed he was picking up on her emotions. She had snapped at him more than once and hated herself for it, because she was the one with problems. Thinking about it now choked her up and she determined to get her act together before she picked him up from Jenny's later.

Jenny, her next-door-neighbour, had a boy of Tom's age and was happy to look after Tom until Sofie finished work on school days. It was her daughter Annie who babysat for Sofie whenever necessary. It was an ideal situation all round, giving Annie extra pocket money.

Usually her work distracted Sofie from her outside worries,

but not this time. Things were not going well. Lack of sleep was the problem. Right now she was muttering to herself as she worked at enlarging a head and shoulders portrait for a client and the air was turning a delicate blue. She rarely used bad language and, when driven to, used only the mildest of epithets. It was just as well she was momentarily alone in the High Street studio. David was doing a photographic session at a client's home and Jimmie, the apprentice lab assistant, was out getting them some lunch.

Sofie was just in the process of making a fine adjustment when the buzzer sounded. She jumped like a scalded cat, undoing minutes of careful work in one fell swoop, evidence of how shot her nerves were. The buzzer was simply alerting her to the fact that someone had entered the studio and never had such an effect on her. Cocking an ear, she waited to hear Jimmie call out that it was only him, but silence reigned, meaning it must be a customer.

Abandoning her work, she started to unbutton her lab coat. Ordinarily a receptionist would be on hand to deal with anyone who walked in off the street, but Tina had called in sick, so she and Jimmie were covering. Hanging her coat on the back of the door, she opened it and stepped out into the studio's reception area.

'Sorry to keep you waiting,' she apologised brightly, although she didn't immediately see anyone. Stepping forward to glance around a corner of the oddly shaped room, she saw the rear view of a man standing before one of the photographs which lined the walls. He had his hands in his trouser pockets and appeared to be studying it intently. Her nerves jangled for a second time in as many minutes as she registered that special charge in the air and knew who her visitor was. Lucas had finally come calling.

'No problem. I'm a very patient man. I've always been prepared to wait as long as I had to to get what I wanted,' he said pointedly as he turned to face her. 'I've been studying your photos. They're very good. You have a knack of bringing out the true person behind the face.'

Sofie had to admit to being surprised by his compliment, but it would have meant more had he not delivered the promise of retribution first. However, it was more comfortable to concentrate on the photographs until he was ready to say what he had clearly come to say.

'They aren't all mine,' she pointed out stiffly. She didn't generally take the photos in the studio because that was her boss's job. However, he had been impressed with her private work and had insisted that some of them should adorn the walls of the studio.

Lucas nodded thoughtfully. 'I know. This one, that one, and the two over there, are,' he said as he pointed to them. 'I recognise your style. There's a depth to them that the others lack.'

She wouldn't be human if she wasn't pleased by his praise. 'I try to make every picture tell a story.'

'You've succeeded remarkably well. Seeing beyond the obvious was always one of your talents. Not one of your hidden ones, though,' he drawled ironically, a comment that made her tense up as the gloves came off.

'What hidden talents do I have?' she felt compelled to ask, and he smiled.

'Why, the ability to vanish without trace, of course,' he retorted, and Sofie decided that was enough false politeness.

'What can I do for you, Lucas?' she asked with all the composure she could muster.

Yet, whilst outwardly she appeared businesslike, on the inside her heart had another agenda. She couldn't help eating him up with her eyes. There had been a time when she would have walked up to him, slid her arms around him and ignited the passion which was never far from the surface. Those days were long gone. She couldn't imagine him wanting her touching him now. Nevertheless, she balled her hands into fists, lest temptation get the better of her, schooling her expression into one that, hopefully, gave little away.

Lucas came a little closer, a mocking smile curving his lips, blue eyes glinting. 'Quite a lot, as I recall, *amore,*' he declared in the sexy undertone she remembered so well but had never thought to hear from him again. Just like years ago, it sent shivers up and down her spine.

As he spoke, those mesmerising eyes ran over her with deliberate provocation, making her feel as if he had actually touched her, though there was virtually the width of the room between them. Her nervous system shot into overdrive and every hair on her body rose up. It was still an incredible sensation and made her feel weak at the knees.

Yet it was totally inappropriate, considering the circumstances, and Sofie battled to keep her reaction from showing, because she knew his look was a taunt to test her responses. He was toying with her and she couldn't allow him to see how he still had the power to affect her so strongly.

'Back in the day, maybe, but not now,' she declared stolidly, forcing her legs to propel her to the desk, where she was able to lean against it and take the weight off her trembling knees.

Hands still in pockets, he strolled towards her, and she was made vitally aware of the strength and power in those long legs and muscular thighs. She could recall in minute detail how they felt wrapped around hers and it set a pulse throbbing way down inside her. She very nearly groaned and willed herself to stop her thoughts from taking that wayward path.

'Why not? After all, nothing has changed between us,' he countered smoothly, the words ricocheting through her system, setting her stomach turning.

Her eyes widened. What game was he playing now? What could he possibly hope to achieve by going down this road? Clearing a throat that showed a disconcerting tendency to dry up at his staggering claim, she managed to speak. 'I left you. That would be called a change.'

'True, but I discovered something interesting the other night. Despite my feelings about what you did, that connection between us was still there. Across the clichéd crowded room, it was as hot and as powerful as ever. It's not over, is it, *caro?*' Lucas challenged softly, setting her pulse racing madly.

Sofie staggered mentally and flipped open the appointment book with trembling fingers, pretending to read it. This was a tack she had never thought he would take. He couldn't mean anything by it; it was just a means of rattling her chain. And he *was* rattling it—violently. 'D-don't be ridiculous. Everything was over when I left. I told you the other evening it was a waste of time pursuing this.' She made herself glance up at him. 'Look, I'm too busy for this. Do you want David to take your picture?' she asked curtly, and the gleam in his eyes grew more intense.

'That too.'

Her nerves leapt so much it must have been visible. Concurrently, anger suddenly welled up and she looked him squarely in the eye. 'Stop it, Lucas! This isn't funny. I don't have time for your games. In fact, I think you should leave right now!'

'Who said it was a game? You and I have plenty of unfinished business between us. More than I imagined. So, I won't be going anywhere just yet. Let's say I plan to investigate the possibilities more fully. Besides, you used to want to be alone with me,' he confided, still with just the faintest hint of mocking amusement in his tone.

She stared at him, her large green eyes incredulous. 'Let me see if I have this straight. You're telling me you still want me and you think I want you too?' He was quite right, of course. The pull of sexual attraction was so incredibly strong she felt shivery and had to battle a primal instinct which was urging her to close the distance between them. It was taking all her strength to remain where she was.

Lucas laughed. 'I don't think, *caro,* I know. There was always this powerful chemistry between us. I felt it the instant I saw you again, and so did you.'

Also true, but once again she refused to admit it. 'Don't presume to know me.'

'Can any man truly know a woman? Look at my own situation. I thought I knew you, but I never suspected that you would just up and leave the way you did. However, when it comes to recognising physical attraction, I'm never wrong. You still want me, Sofie. If I kissed you right now, you'd melt in my arms just as you always did.'

She couldn't withhold a gasp at his sheer gall, true though she knew it to be. 'You have a n-nerve!' she protested, and he laughed out loud.

'Actually I have thousands and, though I would wish it otherwise, they're all responding to you! Urging me to kiss you. To answer the mystery of how those luscious lips would taste now.'

Naturally, that drew her eyes to *his* lips, and all her senses suddenly wanted to know the taste and feel of them again. 'If you *tried* to kiss me, I'd slap your face!'

'No, you wouldn't,' he argued with conviction, and her pulse jumped because, of course, he was right.

Which was why she couldn't allow it to go unchallenged. 'And you know this because…'

His answer was to step closer so he could reach out and touch the pulse that beat at the base of her throat. Sofie felt the contact to the very core of her. It was like getting a powerful electric charge that sent shockwaves rippling through her. Her breath caught as he looked deeply into her eyes.

'Your pulse is racing, *caro,*' he declared mockingly.

She brushed his hand away. 'Of c-course it is. I'm angry with you!' she stammered, and his lips curved into a broader smile.

'Liar,' he countered softly. 'If you were truly angry, you would be sending out totally different vibrations, giving an altogether different message.'

'I'm not sending any message!' she retorted gamely, all the while floundering in this totally unexpected situation.

'You might not want to be, but you are. I know all the subliminal signals you send out. Your message is as clear as if you had used neon lights!' he told her confidently, and her stomach lurched nervously. She didn't want him to know her so well. She needed him to be blinded by anger. Only then could she be sure of keeping her secret hidden.

Unable to retreat from the field he had chosen to fight on, she folded her arms across her chest and squared up to him. 'Th-that's one heck of an ego you've got,' she returned derisively.

Lucas shrugged, unfazed by her claim. 'What you call ego, I call simple honesty. If you weren't attracted to me, why were you watching me so ravenously the other night?'

Sofie caught her breath at his choice of words. 'I was looking at a lot of people,' she corrected firmly, though her voice held the faintest of wobbles.

'Indeed you were, but none of them did you watch as you watched me,' he countered boldly. 'So much hidden passion, *caro!* It begs the question, why did you leave me when you still want me so much after all this time?'

He had given her an opening and she used it. 'Yes, well… s-sex isn't everything,' she said as she struggled to find something else to say. When they came, they were painfully hard words to utter. 'W-when I realised there was…nothing else going for us, I…I left.' Oh, she ought to be struck down for the lie! She had wanted everything from him—she still did. However, her distrust would never let her risk her heart again.

If her answer stung, he didn't show it. In response he raised his eyebrows. 'Really? And yet I have the distinct memory of you telling me I was the love of your life,' he said softly, and his blue gaze lanced into hers, testing her reaction.

Sofie had to brace herself to look him in the eye. 'I must have lied,' she denied croakily, and it hurt to say it, because he was, and always would be, her only love. 'I s-suppose I wanted you to ask me to marry you out of sheer vanity. Y-you were quite a catch, you know.' She watched him for signs of anger, but he was too much in control to reveal anything. She couldn't begin to guess what he was thinking.

'If I was that much of a catch, why leave the goose that lays the golden egg?'

She managed to shrug, pretending an indifference she could never feel. Of course she hadn't married him for his money, though if it would speed his departure she would allow him to think so. Fortunately she had an answer ready. 'I didn't want to be trapped that way.'

That brought a sardonic twist to his lips. 'How unlucky for you, because you're still trapped, *caro*. The marriage wasn't dissolved and, as you left me, the matter of divorce is in my hands.'

'Then let me go,' she urged in a flash, willing him to agree.

Lucas tipped his head on one side thoughtfully. 'You know,

caro, I would, were it not for one thing. I'm not ready to let you go yet.'

Anxiety brought a lump to her throat and she had to swallow hard. 'B-but you have to!'

He laughed, a far from pleasant sound, revealing at last some of the anger inside him. 'I have to do nothing. I have control here, Sofie. You signed up for the whole nine yards. I don't think a couple of months is much of a bargain. As I said, you owe me, and I fully intend to collect—in kind.'

Sofie's heart contracted and her breath failed her. 'Y-you can't possibly be suggesting that you and I…' The words wouldn't form, but she knew what he was proposing—that she return to the marriage bed until he said enough. 'That's positively medieval! I—I'd have to be crazy to agree!'

Lucas shrugged. 'On the contrary, it would be crazy to refuse—if you want your freedom.'

Sofie stared at him, hardly crediting what she was hearing. The man she had fallen in love with would never have suggested such a thing. But then, she hadn't believed that he would ever betray her, either.

'I will never give in to blackmail. You and I getting back together for any reason can never happen,' she responded tautly, attempting to regain control of the situation.

'Never say never, Sofie. It's tantamount to a challenge, or is that what you intended all along?'

Her nerves skittered because that hadn't been her intention at all. 'Why would I challenge you? I want you out of my life, not back in it!' He had to go—for more than one reason. She couldn't allow him to find out about Tom, and she couldn't let him try to work his magic on her—she was far too susceptible to it.

'That, I'm afraid, is unlikely to happen any time soon.

However, let me get to the point of my visit and leave you alone for the rest of the afternoon. I came to tell you I shall be taking you to dinner this evening.'

Sofie's stomach leapt at the blunt statement of intent, but at least it stirred her sleeping temper. 'You came to tell me? What if I have other plans?' she challenged angrily, but Lucas was unmoved.

'Cancel them,' he commanded shortly, and they were staring at each other like protagonists in a ring when the telephone rang.

'Shall I take the call or would that interfere with your plans?' she asked sarcastically, which brought a mocking smile to his lips.

'By all means take the call,' he insisted calmly, making her blood boil.

Muttering under her breath at his cavalier tactics, she reached for the receiver. 'Hello?' she greeted the caller, hoping that if it turned out to be a long call Lucas might leave.

'Hi, gorgeous, why haven't you rung me?' challenged a familiar voice, and Sofie laughed affectionately, half turning away from Lucas for a little privacy, as the man on the other end of the line was Nick Colclough, a local gallery owner who was trying to persuade her into putting on a show of her work. So far she had refused.

'Sorry, Nick, but I've been busy. You know how it is. How was the trip?' Nick had been holidaying in the Bahamas with his family.

'Incredible. Let's have lunch and I'll tell you all about it,' he suggested cheerfully.

'Can't, I'm afraid, I'm having a working lunch today,' she refused truthfully.

'Dinner, then. I've had an idea about a combined showing

that might tempt you into saying yes. We need to talk it over,' Nick urged her to agree, and Sofie was tempted to accept just to put Lucas's nose out of joint. However caution prevailed.

'Could we make it lunch tomorrow? I have…plans for tonight,' she told him, glancing over her shoulder at Lucas, who, she discovered, was watching her intently.

'With anyone I know?' Nick responded cheekily, and Sofie laughed wryly.

'It's just business,' she corrected, wishing it really were that simple. 'See you tomorrow, Nick. Bye.' She ended the conversation and set the receiver back down.

'Boyfriend trouble?' Lucas asked casually when she turned back to him, and Sofie sighed heavily, combing her hair back with her fingers.

'Nick's a friend, nothing more,' she retorted tiredly. Her lack of sleep was catching up with her, shortening her temper when she really needed to be cool and controlled.

One eyebrow lifted. 'Really? Does he know that?'

She looked at him squarely, eyes flashing angrily. 'Nick is a happily married man. Our relationship, such as it is, is strictly professional,' she informed him firmly.

Lucas merely nodded. 'Good, because for the foreseeable future you won't be seeing other men,' he said bluntly, and now it was her turn to raise her eyebrows.

'Just because we're still technically married, don't think you can order me about,' she warned him, and those blue eyes took on a challenging glitter.

'You misunderstand me. It was a statement, not an order. You won't be seeing other men because you won't want to,' he corrected in a voice as smooth as velvet and, though she wasn't about to say so, she knew full well that Lucas was more than enough for any woman.

However, it would only count if she were about to comply with his wishes, and she wasn't that foolish. 'Well, now,' Sofie said doggedly, folding her arms, 'we'll have to see about that, won't we?'

It was a challenge no red-blooded man could ignore and Lucas stepped closer, so that every increasingly ragged breath she took brought with it the spice of his cologne mixed with his unique scent. 'Do you doubt it?'

She inhaled deeply and incredibly had the urge to close her eyes and savour it. 'It's beside the point. I have no intention of playing your games!'

At that he smiled with lazy confidence. 'Then it's up to me to get you to change your mind,' he countered, not about to take no for an answer. Flicking back his cuff, he glanced at his wrist-watch. 'I have to go. I shall pick you up at eight. Don't be late.'

Sofie blinked at the sudden change to brisk businessman. 'I haven't said I was going to have dinner with you,' she reminded him.

'No, but we both know you are. Besides, you put Nick off for me,' he came back swiftly and she gritted her teeth, reluctantly accepting he had won the point.

'You don't know where I live.'

His beautiful lips twitched. 'Don't I? You'd be surprised what I've discovered about you in the last couple of days, Sofie,' he told her, and immediately icy fingers tightened about her heart as she contemplated what that might be. 'You live in a cottage in a village just outside the city. You started working here a couple of years ago and have a small bank account, but no credit card, under the name of Talbot. How am I doing so far?'

Sofie felt giddy with relief. He knew nothing about Tom! 'It's amazing what money can do!' she retorted snappily.

'Why the name Talbot? You never quite explained that.'

She didn't want to explain it now either, but it occurred to her that if she wanted him to stop digging it would be in her best interests to give him some facts herself. 'After my Grandma Talbot, on my mother's side. She was the one who got me interested in photography.'

'We never did get around to talking about our families, did we? We were far too busy making love,' Lucas pointed out ironically. 'Now, I really must go. Until tonight. And Sofie…' he gave her a penetrating look '…don't even think about backing out.'

With that word of warning, he finally strode out of the studio, leaving Sofie to collapse on to the seat behind the desk and prop her head in her hands. She couldn't believe what had just passed between them. Lucas had to be crazy to think she would ever agree to his plan for them. He might have a right to be angry at her leaving without giving him a chance to defend himself, but the payment he demanded was going too far!

She rubbed her hands over her face, trying to think. There had to be something she could do to get him to change his mind. Whatever she did, it had to be tonight, for she couldn't have him lingering around her in case he would find out about Tom.

Tom! Her stomach lurched as she realised that her son would be at home when Lucas called for her. If he should see him, then he was far too astute a man not to realise that Tom was his. The consequences of him knowing were too great. She couldn't lose her son. It would destroy her. Battening down on a rising sense of panic, she knew she must keep Tom hidden.

Reaching for the telephone, she dialled a number and

shortly a familiar voice answered. 'Hi, Jenny, it's Sofie. I have a really big favour to ask you…'

Minutes later she set the receiver back on its cradle and took a calming breath. It was all arranged. Now all she had to do was survive the rest of the evening.

CHAPTER THREE

THAT evening Sofie felt able to take a long, hopefully relaxing bath, secure in the knowledge that Tom was staying over at Jenny's house and would never know that Lucas had been and gone. Her conscience troubled her, though. Having discovered she was pregnant after leaving Lucas, there had been a good reason not to tell him about the baby. Not to tell him now felt wrong, but she had lied herself into a corner. It was fear of what Lucas would say, what he would do, that sealed her lips now.

It was this uneasy conscience which finally killed what small hopes she had had of relaxing and before long she climbed out, wrapping herself in one towel and her hair in another, before padding back into her bedroom to survey her wardrobe.

There were few dresses to choose from, as her budget hadn't allowed her the range of clothes she had once owned. With a young child in the house, she had tended to go for serviceable, not fancy clothes. However, she wanted to set the right mood. A suit would be too formal and anything remotely sexy was a non-starter. She didn't want Lucas to think she had accepted his proposal. In the end she decided on a turquoise-blue layered chiffon confection with a beaded top and tiny straps. She'd had it for years, but it was ideal for the purpose. Barely there, it moved around her even in the softest breeze.

She still had the matching sandals and an evening purse and knew it would be perfect. The whole ensemble was elegant but not too inviting.

All remained then was to dry her hair, which she did, leaving it falling in a gentle curve to her shoulders, and apply a little make-up. By that time it was getting late and she quickly slipped on her underwear, stepped into the dress and was just finishing fastening the straps of her sandals when the doorbell rang.

With one last glance in the mirror to make sure everything was as she wanted it, Sofie went downstairs. She didn't rush, needing to appear calm and composed for what she knew would not be a comfortable evening, but that went out of the window the instant she opened the door.

If she had thought Lucas was handsome the other evening, then tonight was a real eye-opener. He was wearing a tuxedo that had clearly been made for him and the sight of him had her heart doing crazy flip-flops in her chest. She didn't love him for his looks, but seeing him this way brought an upsurge of her feelings for him. She loved him so very much and it hurt not to be able to tell him so. He looked magnificent and quite simply took her breath away.

Lucas was right when he'd told her nothing had changed. He still had the power to make her go weak at the knees, and would no doubt be able to do so when they were both old and grey. Even her mouth went dry and all the tiny hairs on her body stood to attention.

'Breathtaking,' Lucas declared the very next instant, his eyes taking in the gentle curves of her figure outlined by her dress.

The sound of his voice brought her back to a sense of reality and the realisation that to keep him standing on the doorstep might draw unwelcome attention from the neighbours. As would the fancy limousine outside the gate. She hadn't anticipated that, and hoped Tom wasn't looking out of the window next door.

It was the very last thing she wanted and, dragging in some much needed air, Sofie gathered her scattered wits. 'Come in,' she invited hastily, stepping back to allow him to walk inside, which he did, leaving a trace of that same cologne she had enjoyed from their very first meeting. She closed her eyes for a moment, swaying at yet another upsurge of bittersweet memories, then immediately told herself to get a grip. The past was another country and she could never go back there. Closing the door, she steadied herself before following in his wake.

Lucas had come to a halt in the middle of her living room and was surveying its comfortable, lived-in look. She was thankful she'd had the foresight to put all Tom's toys and photos away before Lucas had arrived. Now he turned towards her, pulling a flat square box from his pocket.

'This is for you,' he declared, holding it out to her.

She took it with a deep sense of unease and knew why when she recognised the name of a prestigious jeweller embossed on the top. Sofie immediately offered it back to him. 'I can't take it,' she refused thickly, her throat closing over with conflicting emotions.

Lucas's eyes glittered mockingly. 'Why not? It's yours. I bought it for you on the day you left me. I wanted to give you a token of how much I loved you. Of course, that was when I believed you felt the same. However, a gift is a gift, and nobody else will ever wear it. Open it, *caro*. It won't bite.'

Sofie didn't want to, but to refuse would only make him curious, so she acceded. Her fingers were trembling when she opened the box and saw what was inside. A single teardrop diamond hung from a fragile-looking diamond necklace. She was stunned by the gift and for a moment could say nothing. This was a love token, bought on the very day she had left him. She could only imagine the feelings that must have gone through him when he'd returned to their home to find her gone. Diamonds were many things to many people, but to most they were a gift of love. As enduring as time. It would have meant so much to her then that it brought her to the point of tears now.

'I can't possibly accept this!' she exclaimed in a choked voice. 'Take it back, please.'

Smiling faintly, Lucas reached over but, instead of taking back the box as she expected, he merely removed the necklace. Fire shot around the room as light caught the facets. 'I knew the instant I saw this necklace whose neck it had to grace,' he said conversationally as he walked behind her and slipped the delicate piece of work around her neck, fastening it with ease. 'Of course, I was blinded by my love for you, but no matter. You cured me quickly enough. I was right about it suiting you, though,' he added, stepping back to admire the setting.

'No, no, no!' Sofie exclaimed, her free hand lifting to seek out the fastener and remove the necklace. 'This is wrong. Take it off, please,' she urged him when her fingers failed to work the clasp because they were trembling too much.

In response Lucas folded his arms and shook his head. 'Leave it where it is, for tonight at least. After that you can do with it what you please, because I cannot and will not take it back.'

Sofie stared at him in consternation. 'You're crazy!' she gasped, watching as he shrugged.

'For wanting to give my beautiful wife a beautiful necklace? I don't think anyone will lock me up for that,' he returned dryly. 'Leave it on, Sofie. Think of it as a small penance. Something to take off the balance of what you owe me.'

Of course, as soon as he said that, what else could she do but give in? She would do anything to get him to leave. Though, in her heart of hearts, she would always wish things were different and they could be together for ever, he had to go. However painful they were, the choices had been made and she must live with them. Sighing heavily, she closed the empty box and ran her fingers over the gem she could feel against her skin. 'Very well, but only for tonight. I wouldn't dare wear it again. It must have cost a small fortune!' she observed uncomfortably.

He laughed softly. 'My grandfather taught me that a gentleman would never be so indelicate as to mention money. However, if you're worrying if I could afford it, have no fears. It's a mere drop in the ocean, compared to the family fortune.'

The Antonetti dynasty was a byword in financial circles for good business sense; however, they were also one of the most philanthropic, doing much good work to help the less fortunate. 'How are your parents?' she enquired awkwardly, knowing that, as much as she liked them and they her, they would not have approved of her behaviour. 'Have you told them about meeting me?'

'My parents are both well, and no, I haven't mentioned meeting you. They took your leaving badly, you know, because they had come to consider you as a daughter. It's no wonder they were at a loss to comprehend how you could do what you did. You disappointed them.' Lucas didn't bother to pull his punches and her conscience smote her, even though it had been his behaviour that caused her to leave.

Sofie drew in a ragged breath. 'I'm sorry about that, but it couldn't be helped,' she replied unhappily, which made him laugh wryly.

'No, they just happened to be innocent bystanders who got

caught in the aftermath of your arbitrary decision,' he jibed caustically and, had she not needed to keep quiet for her son's sake, she might well have thrown his own actions back at him.

'I'd rather not talk about it,' she declared tersely, and grim lines settled around his mouth.

'No, of course you wouldn't. It's easier that way. Nothing to bother your conscience…, supposing you have one in the first place. However, I didn't come here to talk about my family. At least, not right now. Are you ready to go? I have a table booked for eight-thirty.'

Sofie glanced at the clock on the mantelpiece and saw it was already ten past eight. 'I just have to get my purse. If you want something to drink, help yourself from the cupboard,' she pointed to one in the corner.

'I'll wait until later,' he refused politely. 'Take your time. I'm going to enjoy the view of your garden.'

Sofie left him looking out of the window and returned to her bedroom, where she sank on to her dressing table stool and stared at her reflection. Immediately her eyes were caught by the diamond necklace and she had to admit it *was* beautiful. Her throat closed over. He had seen it and thought of her, and it brought her to the verge of tears again. What a fool she was. Lucas had been the one at fault, and yet here she was falling apart because he had bought her a necklace. She was crazy to still love him, though he had played her false. Yet she couldn't help herself. Which was why wearing the necklace, that would once have meant so much, was almost physically painful. However, it was a small price to pay, and if it got him to leave, so much the better. As for anything else, he was going to be disappointed. There could be nothing between them now, not even to salve his pride. She dared not, in case she revealed just how much she cared.

With her emotions back in control and her sense of purpose restored, Sofie was finally ready to go back downstairs. She checked her appearance one last time, told herself she could get through this, retrieved her evening purse and a shawl from the bed and went to rejoin Lucas.

He turned from the window immediately. 'Ready?' he enquired and, when she nodded, held out his arm for her to take.

She raised an eyebrow questioningly, heart lurching. 'That's a little over the top, don't you think?' she challenged, making no move to take his arm. She didn't want to touch him because she craved the closeness that was lost too much. Far better to keep distance between them.

Lucas, however, wasn't about to be gainsaid. 'Humour me,' he told her lightly, but there was something steely in his look that urged her compliance.

'More penance?' she taunted, whilst her heart quailed as she knew she had to give in to the unspoken pressure. Against her will, she slipped her hand into the crook of his arm.

Sensing her reluctance, he tutted mockingly. 'You have a short memory, *caro*. Once you couldn't wait to get your hands on every part of my body,' he goaded, turning her stomach over. Their lovemaking had been exquisite and she'd never forgotten it.

'Maybe I just prefer not to remember my mistakes,' she countered with all the sang-froid she could muster.

Lucas urged her out of the cottage ahead of him and closed the door firmly. 'It's interesting you call it a mistake, as that would mean you're fated to repeat it,' he argued sardonically, and she shot him an equally scornful look.

'Not if I learn from it first.'

Lucas laughed. 'I can see this is going to be quite a battle. I'm looking forward to it already.'

Unlike Sofie, who had come to believe this meeting would never happen. 'Just remember, I'm only agreeing to dinner with you.' It wouldn't hurt to tell him again.

'This time, naturally,' Lucas concurred with a tilt of his head. 'I'm prepared to give you time to get used to the idea. However, restitution will have to be made eventually. One of the reasons for taking you to dinner was to discuss terms.'

Sofie's heart contracted as he talked about a resumption of their relationship as if it were a business deal. 'One of the reasons?' she probed in what she hoped was a steady voice.

'We have a lot to talk about. The whys and wherefores, so to speak.'

Not if she could help it! 'All I can say is I hope you're prepared for a one-sided conversation.'

'Don't worry, *amore,* after the way you walked out on me, I'm prepared for anything.'

A chauffeur climbed from the waiting limousine as they approached it and Sofie silently prayed that nobody would notice and tell Tom tomorrow. Lucas helped her into the back before joining her. Clearly the driver already had his instructions, for no sooner were they buckled in than he drove off.

'Where are we going?' she asked, when they didn't head back into the city but took a route that led to the coast.

'A colleague recommended a restaurant overlooking the sea not too far away. I thought we'd go there. The fish is supposed to be excellent. Kind of reminds me of the first time I met you. At that seafood restaurant on the quayside in Bali. Do you remember it?'

Of course she remembered it. Nothing about their time together was forgotten. She had been holidaying with a group of friends, one of whom had been pestering her, trying to take their friendship to an altogether different level—one Sofie hadn't wanted to go. So she had left the table and wandered down to the end of the pier. That was where Lucas had found her a short time later.

'You should have blacked his eye,' he declared, coming to lean on the wooden rail beside her.

She turned and looked into a pair of the most brilliant blue eyes she had ever seen and fell under their spell in the blink of an eyelid. Her, 'Excuse me?' was more to give herself a moment to recover than because she hadn't heard.

Lucas smiled, sending her heart reeling. 'Your friend. I hope you don't intend to treat me that way.'

Sofie raised her eyebrows, then laughed softly. 'Aren't you being rather premature? You and I are nothing to each other.'

'No,' he confirmed lazily, 'but we will be.'

Turning slightly, she rested her weight against the wooden rail, more than a little staggered that her knees were getting weak beneath her. 'Don't I have any say in this?'

He turned to face her, all casualness and male grace. 'Of course you do. The where and when is up to you.'

'But not the if?'

His blue eyes travelled lazily over her face and she felt the warmth of them like a touch. 'There is no if. We both know that.'

Sofie drew in an unsteady breath. 'Does this approach usually work for you?'

His smile lit a fire deep inside her. 'I don't have a "one size fits all" approach. I adapt it to suit the woman in question.'

'And you think your chosen line is working with me?' she charged him, not about to confirm that it was.

'Of course. You're intrigued and want to know more.'

'What intrigues me is your name,' she returned smoothly. 'You do have one, I take it?'

'Lucas Antonetti,' he introduced himself. 'And you are Sofie Palmer. I asked one of your friends,' he explained, seeing her surprise.

It excited her to know how much he had wanted to meet her, but she kept that to herself. 'You're not some escaped lunatic, are you?' she teased lightly and his response took her breath away.

'Not yet, though you certainly have the ability to drive a man mad,' he countered lazily.

Sofie laughed and quirked an eyebrow at that. 'Are you telling me you think I'm a tease?'

His eyes flashed with wicked humour. 'You tell me. Do you always deliver what your eyes promise?'

She shrugged one elegant shoulder. 'That would depend on what they're promising. I've been told they spit fire when I'm angry, but I've never set anyone alight,' she revealed lightly, and was fascinated by the way his eyes seemed to gleam with hidden thoughts.

'Now that I don't believe. When your eyes send out those scintillating flames of passion they must burn a man right up,' he argued in a husky tone that sent shivers down her spine.

There was no way she could prevent her breath from catching at that. 'Do you always say exactly what you're thinking?' she gasped, surprisingly disconcerted by his forwardness.

'Only if the situation is appropriate. Right now I couldn't possibly tell you everything that's going through my mind. For that we would have to be quite alone.'

Sofie silently acknowledged that he was good at this. She couldn't recall feeling such an intense attraction before. He had the kind of charisma she found intensely exciting.

'So, Lucas Antonetti, should I know of you?'

'That would depend on how familiar you are with the

world of international big business,' he returned smoothly and Sofie couldn't resist shooting him a flirtatious look from beneath her lashes.

'So you're a businessman. I'm impressed. I can't say I've been pursued by a businessman before,' she responded with a husky laugh that brought a gleam of something hot and dangerous to his eyes.

'It's a first for both of us. I've never pursued a…' Lucas paused, allowing his gaze to wander over her again. Slowly his lips curved into a wicked smile and his eyes rose to lock with hers. '…Sofie Palmer before.'

Sofie's breathing went awry and she couldn't look away. 'So, where do we go from here?' she asked, her voice sounding oddly scratchy to her own ears.

Eyes twinkling, he sighed ruefully. 'I know where I would like to go, but that would be out of the question.'

She took a shaky breath, not so much staggered by what he had said, as she had heard that suggestion before, but rather her physical response to it, given that her trust in men was at rock bottom. 'Do you always move so fast?'

'When I see something I want, yes,' Lucas confessed huskily. 'However, I can go slowly when the situation demands it,' he added, a roguish twinkle in his eye.

Sofie's heart contracted at the memories, because he had gone slow. For all the passionate attraction they had both felt, she knew now that he had wooed her. They hadn't just tumbled into bed and thought the world well lost. They had waited as long as they could and got to know each other before taking the step both had wanted. It had been…heaven, but all too soon she had had to go home, and there she had thought it would end. Except Lucas thought otherwise, which had led to the most beautiful of weddings and, eventually, the cruellest betrayal.

'Sofie?'

The questioning use of her name now drew Sofie out of the bittersweet reverie she had slipped into. She took in a deep breath as she looked around her. Lucas was watching her broodingly.

'Are we there?' she asked uncomfortably, feeling like a bug under a microscope, from the way he was observing her. It made her wonder if she had somehow said or done something out of place.

'Not far,' Lucas answered, never taking his eyes off her. 'The question is, where were you? You looked miles away.'

Knowing she could hardly tell him what she had really been thinking, even were she inclined to, Sofie made a production out of sitting up straighter and smoothing down her dress. 'The motion of the car was sending me to sleep. I haven't slept well lately.'

One eyebrow lifted mockingly. 'Guilty conscience?'

'Over what I did? Not a jot,' she lied hardily, needing to keep up a firm front. She couldn't allow even the smallest chink in her armour to appear, lest he see through it and make the discovery she feared. 'I wouldn't change a thing.'

Lucas gave a slow shake of his head. 'I had no idea you were so callous. Or maybe I was too besotted to care. Either way, the blinkers are well and truly off. You won't be making a fool of me a second time, *caro.*'

Nor will you make an idiot of me, she thought as she turned to look out of the window. How convenient it was for him to live with a double standard. Doubtless his roving eye was just a male thing, whilst her running off was a heinous crime!

Neither spoke again until the car drew up before the restaurant. It was busy, as its reputation had spread, but they were shown to a quiet table overlooking the sea. Lucas ordered a glass of white wine for Sofie and a whisky for himself. However, it wasn't until these drinks had been brought, their dinner order placed and they were finally alone, that he turned to her. Sofie was unaware that she was restlessly twisting her glass in her fingers, but it didn't escape Lucas.

'Nervous, *amore?*'

The affectionate term struck a nerve, as it was meant to do, though with more force than Lucas would ever expect her to feel. 'I'm not your darling, Lucas. I haven't been that for a long time. Which is why I have no reason to be nervous,' Sofie returned boldly, and that brought a dangerous-looking smile to his lips. 'Why don't you just get on with whatever it is you intend to do?'

Lucas sat back and calmly crossed one leg over the other. 'Very well. Let's set the ball rolling. You can start by telling me again why you left me.'

Sofie drew in an unsteady breath, as she had assumed he believed what she had told him earlier today. His question suggested otherwise, and left her floundering. 'D-does it matter? It's in the past.'

For once he allowed the true depth of his anger to show. 'Oh, it matters, *caro.* You trampled my pride in the dust when you walked out that way. The very least that you owe me is an *honest* explanation.' The stress he placed on the word meant he didn't believe he had heard one yet.

Nor was he about to. The truth, like so much else, had to remain hidden. She stared at him, brazening it out. 'And if I don't have one?'

The lips that could kiss her with devilish mastery took on an unpleasant twist. 'You're becoming an accomplished liar. Make another one up. When you get close to the truth, I'll know.'

That stung, as it was meant to do and, because his persistence was agitating her, Sofie snatched at the first thought which entered her head. 'OK, you want a reason. How's this? I got bored,' she retorted smartly. 'Does that make you feel better?'

Lucas smiled broadly, not a whit put out. 'Not at all. I know women, and you were never bored whilst you were with me,' Lucas returned confidently and she drew in a sharp breath at his assurance.

Anger began to simmer inside her, momentarily overcoming her anxieties. 'You know that's the most arrogant thing I've ever heard you say! I was not…am not…like all women!'

He leant forward at that, his eyes boring into hers. 'No, you were special. I would have given up the world for you!' he informed her passionately, bringing choking tears to her throat.

'I never asked you for the world!' All she had wanted was to be able to trust him, and in that he had failed her. What did that say about his love? Had it not been for Tom, she would have challenged him there and then. Caution kept her quiet.

'No, *caro,*' Lucas retorted with a harsh laugh. 'However, when you love someone it comes with the territory. If you had loved me as you said you did, you would have known that!'

She almost laughed, because of course she knew. She had loved him so much—still loved him beyond all rhyme or reason—and would have given him everything it was in her power to give. Maybe he had loved her once, but it hadn't been strong enough to stop him seeing another woman. Maybe she should have stayed and faced him with it, but she hadn't. Maybe he would have still loved her in his fashion, but it would have been, oh, so hard to bear. To live in doubt had not been an option. Which made his anger hard to swallow.

Sofie pushed her chair back, preparing to get up. 'I cannot do this. It's crazy. You have to let it go, Lucas. You have to let me go!' she insisted thickly, making to rise, but Lucas shot out a hand and caught her wrist.

'But that I cannot do, *amore*,' he declared in a low intense voice. 'As I told you earlier, I've discovered I still want you and, what is more, before I return home, I fully intend to have you!'

CHAPTER FOUR

THE bold statement of intent momentarily took Sofie's breath away, but when she sank back on to her chair she was ready to do battle. 'Understand this. I'm not going to have any sort of relationship with you.' She refuted the idea in a tight, clipped voice. 'Now let me go.'

Lucas ignored the command and instead turned her hand over in his, beginning a gentle stroking of her palm with his thumb. 'I'm not asking for a lifetime commitment this time. We both know you're incapable of that. But what's a week or two out of the rest of your life, if it will give you your freedom?' he cajoled in that rich dark chocolaty voice which had always melted her resistance and even now sent goose-bumps up her spine.

It was oh, so very tempting. She would be lying to herself if she didn't admit it. To have time with Lucas again, when she had thought all possibility of it had passed, would be the closest thing to heaven, but ultimately it would leave her with nothing. Besides, how could she possibly keep Tom hidden that long? She felt guilty enough about it already.

His touch was sending warmth along her veins, but she resisted pulling her hand away. 'That isn't going to work.' She fought back stoically, knowing she must not let him get under her skin and seduce her. She had to be strong—for Tom.

His lips twitched. 'Liar. You might not want to be responding, but you are,' Lucas insisted, and she would have given anything to be able to prove him wrong.

'Y-you're mistaken.'

He smiled lazily. 'Am I? I think not. I could prove it to you, but that would get us thrown out and I've been looking forward to dining here.'

Sofie had a sudden intense vision of him making love to her on top of the table and felt heat invade her cheeks. Thankfully the lights were low enough to hide the effect of her erotic thought.

'I've never gone in for exhibitionism,' she told him coldly, but that only made him laugh huskily.

'No, but in private you had no inhibitions, I'm happy to say. You were a very passionate and inventive lover. Is it any wonder I want more?'

Memories of their lovemaking crowded into her brain, reminding her of all she had given up. 'We were married then,' she pointed out quickly.

'We're married now,' Lucas retorted swiftly. 'It will all be perfectly legal.'

'Legality isn't the point. I don't want you back in my life, even for a short time,' she told him bluntly, hoping he would give up. Yet she knew he wouldn't. He had been waiting a long time for this and he wasn't about to go away without getting the justice he felt was due him.

Having overloaded her senses with his delicate caress, Lucas finally released her hand and sat back. 'We played it your way. This time I make the rules. You might do well to remember I hold the cards.'

As if his words didn't bother her in the slightest, Sofie

reached for her glass and took a much needed sip of wine before responding. Setting the glass back down, she rested her elbows on the table and her chin on her linked fingers. 'You might think you do, but we both know you cannot stay in the north indefinitely. You have a business to run. So why don't you cut your losses and go home?'

The sardonic glint in his eyes hinted that she was not going to like what he was about to say. 'That would suit you, wouldn't it, *caro?* However, I have no need to rush off as I'm taking a long overdue holiday.'

It was just as well for Sofie that their meal arrived at that moment, because she doubted she would have been able to say anything, so horrified was she by his statement. Her brain felt numb. She had been hoping that he would toy with her for a while, then go back home, but clearly that wasn't about to happen. What on earth was she going to do?

The question kept going round and round in her mind whilst she attempted to eat. As much as she loved seafood, she was unable to do more than pick at her meal. Lucas, on the other hand, had a healthy appetite, and cleared his plate. Which just about put the kibosh on what little appetite she did have. She gave up pretending and pushed the barely touched plate aside.

'Is there something wrong with the food?' Lucas asked considerately. 'I can have them bring something else,' he offered, though they both knew why her appetite had vanished.

'The food was perfect; I just wasn't hungry,' she informed him shortly.

'Hmm, I know how you feel. It isn't much fun when things don't go the way you'd planned. I lost all interest in food when I discovered you had left me,' he confided and her heart twisted painfully.

'I never wanted that to happen,' she apologised as a waiter

appeared to clear away the remains of their meal and Lucas ordered coffee.

'Why would you even give it a thought? You wanted out, so you left. You have to be the abandoned one to understand what I went through,' he added. 'As this appears to be confession time, I'll admit to drinking too much in those first days. Oh, don't worry, I soon realised that wasn't the way. There are no answers in the bottom of a bottle. If I wanted them, I had to find you. Which I tried to do, with no success.'

'I didn't want to be found,' Sofie admitted, as there was little point in saying otherwise. He already knew, despite her earlier denial. He was no fool and she had to remember that.

'Afraid of what I might say or what I might do?'

She sighed heavily. 'Both, I guess. I knew you'd be angry.'

At that Lucas leaned forward across the table. 'You know something, *amore?* Angry is such a tame word for all the feelings seething inside me. I loved you once. I want you still. There's only one way I know to get you out of my system once and for all. I need you back in my bed until this craving I have for you is gone. Only then will I be free of you, and you will be free of me.'

It sounded so simple to him, yet it could never be that. Not only because of Tom—the son he didn't know he had—but because she loved him. That was why she could never agree. 'I can be free now if you would just walk away!' she insisted, willing him to see there was no way she could agree.

Lucas stared at her for a long moment, then shrugged. 'So, it seems we're at an impasse,' he declared, making Sofie frown because he didn't sound the least bit put out by the fact. Lucas meanwhile had signalled the waiter and asked for the bill. As soon as he had paid it, he stood up and walked round to hold her chair so she could do the same.

Confused by this sudden change in tactics, Sofie gathered up her purse and shawl and preceded him out of the restaurant. However, when she made to walk to the car park, Lucas took her by the arm and steered her in the opposite direction, towards the seafront.

'It's early still,' he explained easily. 'I feel like a walk.'

Sofie, who only wanted to go home and end the evening, came to an abrupt halt. 'I don't.'

Lucas looked down at her and quirked an eyebrow. 'Not even if you might learn something to your advantage?'

'What would that be?'

'Ah—' he smiled mockingly '—you'll have to walk with me to find out. Shall we?' He held out his arm for her to take and, after a moment's hesitation, she accepted it. 'There, that wasn't so bad, was it?' he pronounced mockingly as they began walking again.

It was a beautiful evening, enhanced by the gentle tumbling of the waves on the beach. Once upon a time, walking like this would have been perfect, but now all it revealed to Sofie was how desperately alone she felt. She hadn't realised until this moment how painful it could be to be so close to the person you loved and know they no longer loved you. She might wish it were different, but wishing was for children. Grown-ups had to live with the results of their choices.

They had walked far beyond the lights and noise of the restaurant before Lucas broke the silence between them.

'Do you ever think about those first few weeks of our marriage?' he asked her and Sofie's heart turned over.

Only all the time, she thought wistfully. 'I try not to,' she lied. 'I can't imagine why you would want to, either.'

'It helps me keep focused,' he revealed with dry humour. 'Not that I was really likely to forget why I wanted to see you again.'

Sofie had to swallow hard to remove a lump in her throat. 'And has it lived up to your expectations?'

'Pretty much. I expected your resistance, but I thought you would have given in by now,' he admitted, looking down at her to gauge her reaction.

She sent him a mocking look. 'Because you thought I wouldn't be able to resist throwing myself into your arms?' she gibed.

'No,' he denied with a laugh. 'Because it's the easiest solution.'

'For you, maybe, but I can't sleep with someone I have no feelings for,' she returned steadily, knowing that the opposite was actually true for her. She couldn't sleep with him *because* of her feelings.

Lucas came to a halt when he heard that and turned to face her. 'No feelings?' he charged scornfully. 'Doesn't the lie stick in your throat?'

No, but her heart leapt there instantly. Could he have somehow guessed her true feelings? The possibility was petrifying. 'What do you mean?'

'That you want me as much as you ever did,' he reminded her, and relief made her head feel dizzy.

'Physical attraction isn't enough,' she insisted because her aching heart knew lust was no substitute for love.

Lucas, however, saw things differently now. 'It's all I'm interested in, and all I need of you.'

His words were a knife thrust through her heart, even though it was expected. It made her want to find a dark corner somewhere, where she could cry out her pain. 'Well, you're going to be disappointed, as I don't even feel that much!'

Her denial failed to have the desired effect. His smile broadened and he laughed. 'Sofie, Sofie! You should be ashamed. No matter, I can easily prove you wrong,' he declared softly and, stepping forward, used his hand to tilt her head up, before bringing his mouth down on hers.

Caught off guard by the unexpected move, Sofie's senses reeled. His lips were warm and firm and moved over hers with all the longingly remembered expertise that made her shiver. Her hands came up, but if her intent was to push him away they played traitor as her fingers dug into his shoulders. She moaned low in her throat and her mouth parted, allowing him to deepen the kiss. His tongue stroked tantalisingly along the length of her lips, then plunged inside, demanding a response she was compelled to give. Her lashes dropped and she swayed towards him as her senses swam. She could no more resist him than she could hold back the tide. It had always been that way. Her arms slid around his neck and for one blissful moment Lucas's hands tightened on her waist. As if that was the sign he had been waiting for, he finally broke the kiss and stepped back, studying his handiwork with satisfaction.

'I've been wanting to do that since the other night,' he confessed with something akin to a wolfish growl, and Sofie had to stifle an urge to groan out loud. Not from need, but from despair at giving herself away so tamely. Her lashes fluttered upwards and her eyes met smoky blue ones. 'You were saying about not wanting me...' he taunted softly.

From having been adrift on a sensual sea, Sofie had to quickly gather her scattered wits. 'That was a low trick!' she accused with all the scorn she could muster.

Lucas shrugged casually. 'Nevertheless it proved my point. You still want me, Sofie. With all the passion I remember so well.'

Unable to deny it, she raised her chin belligerently. 'It changes nothing!' she insisted, and his expression became set.

'I would think again if I were you.'

Her heart jolted, but there was too much at stake to give in. 'Is that a threat? What can you do if I say no?' she challenged him, and saw his jaw tense.

'You have no idea of what I can do,' he countered in a tone she had never heard him use before.

It sent a chill through her blood. 'No, I don't, but I'm beginning to see a ruthless streak I wasn't aware of,' she shot back cuttingly. 'Does your father have it, too? Is it a case of like father like son? Is that how you do business?' she charged, not caring in that moment if she had gone too far.

Lucas's eyes narrowed. 'What do you mean by that?'

Sofie thought fast. She had been angry and said too much. However she might regret it, it was impossible to take back what she had said, so she might just as well go ahead and use it to her advantage. She was desperate enough to use any means, open or underhand, to get Lucas to go away. Steeling herself, she crossed her arms and faced up to him.

'Big businessmen aren't choirboys. On the contrary, they have to be single-minded and ruthless. Nothing is allowed to stand in the way of what they want. Nothing and nobody!' Having expected to see anger at her attack on his moral fibre, it wasn't surprising when his expression turned steely.

'You're going to have to explain that, *caro,*' he commanded shortly, and she took a deep breath, knowing she had gone too far to back out now.

'How did your company get to be so successful? How many men, like all those people that were in the papers, did your family ruin on their way to the top? How many did they drive to take their own lives?' It was unjust to liken the Antonetti Corporation to the companies which had made headline news just recently, and she knew it, but what else could she do? He couldn't stay up here. He had to be made to leave.

Lucas stared down at her, his face grim and set. 'That's enough! We are nothing like those mongrels and you know it!'

Of course she did, but that wasn't the point right now. 'Do I? What am I to think when you threaten me as you just did?' she questioned, somehow managing to stare him in the eye without flinching.

'Have I ever threatened you with physical harm?' he almost snarled at her.

Sofie raised her chin another notch. 'There's a first time for everything!'

Lucas drew in a ragged breath. 'I have never lifted my hand against a woman. Nor would I ever, no matter what the provocation. I would have sworn you knew that. It just goes to show how wrong I can be. I think I should take you home now.'

Sofie let out a shaky breath as they turned to retrace their steps, this time going straight to the car without attempting to make conversation. She found his silence unnerving and it only added to her sense of unhappiness. If she had won, she had also lost, because she felt wretched inside.

The journey home seemed to take no time at all and it was as they turned into the lane where her cottage was that she had to ask the all important question.

'Will I be seeing you again?'

Lucas glanced round at her. 'There wouldn't be much point, would there? Well done, *caro*. You've got your wish!' he exclaimed sardonically.

It was a bitter victory to Sofie and she climbed out of the car feeling very near to tears. They walked to her gate and she was just turning to Lucas to thank him for dinner when a small commotion down the lane drew their attention.

'Mummy!' a childish, much beloved voice cried out at the same time as a woman's voice.

'There she is, Tom. Didn't I say she wouldn't be long?' Jenny exclaimed lightly and Sofie watched, transfixed, as Jenny hurried down her garden path and came along the lane towards her. 'I'm sorry, Sofie, but Tom was sick and wanted you. The poor little mite has been nigh on inconsolable.' She held the little boy out to his mother and Sofie took him in her arms, her heart turning over as tiny arms and legs fastened around her and a damp cheek pressed into her neck.

'Its OK, darling, Mummy's here,' she reassured him, stroking her hand soothingly over his mop of dark hair. She turned to her neighbour, who had no idea what she had just done, and smiled. 'Its OK, Jenny, I'll take care of him now. Thanks for waiting up with him. I'll see you in the morning.'

She watched her neighbour walk back to her own house and go inside and braced herself to turn and face Lucas. To say he was surprised was an understatement. He was thunderstruck and, even as she watched, she could see the cogs turning in his mind and the truth about who Tom was striking home.

'I'll have to get Tom into bed,' she declared hastily before he could say anything, and headed up the path, rummaging in her purse for her key. An instant later it was taken from her and Lucas quickly produced the key and opened the door. Pushing it wide, he found the light switch and flicked it on.

Sofie spared him another glance and the suppressed emotion in his eyes turned her knees to water. All she could do was concentrate on her son. 'Come on, sweetie, let's get you into your lovely old bed, hmm,' she cooed, mounting the stairs, very much aware of piercing eyes boring into her back.

She had to be calm and comforting for Tom as she put him into bed and covered him up, but her heart was thundering like a mad thing as she realised the enormity of what had just happened. Lucas had seen Tom, and she knew the sky was about to fall in.

Now that he was in his own bed, with his mother close by, Tom quickly fell asleep, leaving Sofie with nothing to do but softly leave the room and go back downstairs where she knew Lucas waited for her. Sure enough she found him in the sitting room, staring out of the window, but with so much tension in his back and shoulders it made her wince. He turned the instant he heard her and his expression was closed.

'How's the boy?' he enquired solicitously, and she swallowed nervously.

'Sleeping. I don't think he'll be sick again. He probably got too excited. You know how children are,' she responded with a shaky little laugh, which faded away under the sternness of his gaze.

'I've very little experience of my own child, as you very well know,' he shot back harshly, and her stomach lurched so much at his choice of words she had to press a hand to it.

Sofie took an unsteady step forward. 'Lucas, I…' She tried to formulate an answer but failed miserably. Not that it mattered, for Lucas had plenty to say.

'Why did you hide him from me?' he demanded, and she could feel his underlying anger.

'I wasn't…' she began, only to be cut off by a hard laugh that made her flinch.

'Don't even try to lie to me, *caro!* What were you afraid of? I wonder. That I would recognise him? Of course you were! You knew the second I saw him I would know he was mine. He's the spitting image of me!' There was so much anger in him he had to pace away to get it under control, then he turned to her again. 'Why did you do it?' The bitterness in his voice brought a painful lump to her throat.

'I didn't know I was pregnant and, when I found out, I thought you wouldn't want to know.'

His jaw flexed as he gritted his teeth. 'Wouldn't want to know? My own child? How could you think I wouldn't care? My own flesh and blood. Damn you, Sofie. How dared you deny him to me?'

Tears burnt her eyes, turning the room into a kaleidoscope, and she brushed them away. 'I thought it was for the best,' she confessed thickly, knowing she had no defence for her actions.

Blue eyes flashed ice at her. 'Who's best? Certainly not mine or the boy's!'

'Tom,' she interposed gruffly. 'His name is Tom. Thomas Luke, after my father and…his.'

That gave Lucas a moment's pause. 'And his given name?'

She licked her lips, her mouth unbelievably dry. 'Officially it's Antonetti. Here we've been using the name Talbot.'

Lucas snorted disgustedly. 'So you couldn't be found. What a pity I happened to have business in the area, or who knows how long it would have been before I discovered the truth?' he exclaimed in outrage.

His anger alarmed her. Not because she feared a physical threat, but what she feared was what he might do now he knew about his son. She looked at him, her heart beating sickeningly fast, whilst her fingers tightened into knots to stop their shaking.

'And now?'

'Now you're right to be afraid. I've only ever been this angry once before, and I came that close to losing it,' he responded, making a tiny gap between thumb and forefinger. 'Say nothing more or, so help me God, I won't be responsible for my actions.'

She had never seen anyone so terribly angry as Lucas was now and, though she wanted to beg and plead for an answer, she knew she had to say nothing. Meanwhile Lucas had paced back and forth from one side of her living room to the other until finally he stopped and dragged faintly trembling hands through his hair.

'I have to get out of here,' he declared abruptly. 'I need to think, and I can't do that here with you. But I'll be back. Make no mistake about that,' he added as he walked to the door. There he paused and looked back at her. 'And Sofie, don't try and run this time. If you do I'll move heaven and earth to find you and you really won't like what will happen then!'

With that warning echoing around the room, he left. Moments later she heard the car start up, then move away. Only then did she sink down on to the nearest chair and drop her head in her hands. Dear God, it was a nightmare! Lucas was so angry, so hurt, and she realised she had never really given any thought to his feelings. She just hadn't wanted him to find out about Tom for fear he would take him from her.

Of course, the instant she let that thought into her brain, panic set in. He was going to take Tom. She just knew it. It would be the perfect punishment for her crime!

Sofie jumped to her feet, the instinctive need to run beating in her brain. Yet that was as far as she got, because she knew she couldn't run. Not this time. There was no place she could hide, now that Lucas knew about Tom. She had to stay and face the music, and that made her feel so incredibly helpless.

Defeated, she sank to her knees as tears ran slowly down her cheeks. Everything was such a mess. After all she had done to make a new life for herself, the cruel fates had decided to take a hand, turning her world upside down. As the tears finally began to slow, Sofie knew that all she could do was wait and pray that she wasn't going to lose everything.

CHAPTER FIVE

IT WAS well into the following afternoon before Sofie finally heard a car come down the lane and stop outside her cottage. She hadn't been to bed, as sleeping had been out of the question. Instead she had spent the night curled up in the corner of the couch, waiting for dawn to break. Then she had gone up to shower and change into cropped trousers and a strappy cotton top. The diamond necklace had been put back in its box and was locked away at the back of her dressing table drawer.

Tom seemed to have recovered and had been his usual cheerful self in the morning and, when given the opportunity of taking the day off, he had insisted he wanted to go to school. Which had suited Sofie, because she hadn't wanted him to overhear her next confrontation with Lucas. She had dropped him off at school, given him a bigger hug than usual, more for her own comfort than for his, which had made him look at her oddly, then she had driven home to await Lucas's arrival.

Having assumed he would turn up early, it did nothing for her nerves that he didn't put in an appearance until the after-noon. Now that he was here, her anxieties were polarized and she went to open the door with a sickening feeling of dread in her stomach. All night she had been playing out scenes in her mind, where he declared his intention of taking Tom away from her and, now that the moment when that scene could well be played out for real was upon her, her bravado crumpled to nothing.

Yet, even under stress, the sight of Lucas made her heart ache. He had dressed down today, wearing jeans and a T-shirt, reminding her so very much of the man she had met and fallen in love with. Apparently he had chosen to drive himself because there was nobody else in the vehicle this time.

As she waited on the doorstep for him to walk up the path, Sofie realised she was twisting her hands into knots and hastily linked her fingers to stop the giveaway signs of her nervousness. The closer he got to her, it was easier to see his expression and, to her dismay, it was closed and tight. Not that she had expected anything else, but she had hoped for a little softness.

'So you decided to heed my warning and stay,' he remarked dryly as soon as he reached her, and Sofie drew in an audibly shaky breath.

'There was no point in running now,' she answered as steadily as she could, and a tight smile curved his lips.

'Now I know about my son, no,' he agreed grimly. 'Where is he, by the way? Hiding out next door?' he asked with a jerk of his head towards her neighbour's house.

Knowing his scorn was justified, Sofie didn't rise to the bait. 'Tom went to school. And, before you say anything, I wanted to keep him off, but he insisted. He'll be home in a little while,' she added with a glance at her wrist-watch. 'Come through to the kitchen,' she invited. 'I'll make us some coffee. Unless you would prefer tea?' She threw that over her shoulder as she led the way through the cottage to her kitchen.

'Coffee's fine,' Lucas said as followed her, taking up a strategic position, leaning his hips against a dresser from where he could watch her go about the task. Sofie filled up the coffee-maker and set it on to drip. Then, as there was nothing to do but wait, she turned to face the man who was still her husband.

For a moment they stood watching each other like combatants waiting for the moment to strike the first blow. It was Lucas who spoke first.

'Did you get any sleep last night?' he asked curtly, and it was a reluctant caring, born out of good manners more than real concern for her well-being.

'No,' Sofie responded with a swift shake of her head. 'You?'

'Not a wink. After what you told me, my mind was going round like a tape stuck in a loop. I kept wondering how I could have been mistaken in you. Now I realise you never loved me. You couldn't and do what you did. I really was just a means to an end, wasn't I? You deserved an Oscar for the act you put on,' he added with a humourless laugh.

Sofie tensed immediately because her reasons for leaving paled into insignificance when faced with the situation now. 'I don't want to talk about that!' she insisted in a choked voice.

Lucas inclined his head in agreement. 'Neither do I, as it happens, but one day we're going to have a serious conversation about it, whether you like it or not. Right now, though, all I'm interested in is my son. You gave him my name, which I suppose I should be grateful for, but what else did you tell him about me? More lies, *caro?*'

Understanding his need to hit back at her didn't make his words easier to take. Especially when she knew he wouldn't like her answer. Feeling ultra-vulnerable, she rubbed her hands up and down her arms as if chilled. 'I told him that you and I didn't live together because…because we didn't love each other any more. And…' Catching a glimpse of the look in his eye, she cleared her throat nervously. 'And that his daddy didn't visit because he was busy going off around the world on business.'

Lucas shook his head in disbelief. 'Very clever. You covered all the bases.'

The sense of guilt she had always carried with her swelled up inside her and made her eyes burn with unshed tears. 'I know I should have told you about him, but I honestly didn't think you would even look for me. Which is why I told Tom, when he was old enough to ask about his father, that maybe one day he would get to meet you,' she added hastily.

'Keeping your fingers crossed as you said it, and hoping the day would never come!' he retorted cuttingly. 'Unfortunately for you, that day has arrived and, I tell you now, I fully intend to get to know my son!'

Which was what she had always known the man she loved would want to do. Licking dry lips, Sofie gave him the only answer she could. 'I know. I'm not going to stand in your way,' she told him huskily. Suddenly the tears threatened to overflow as her emotions see-sawed with her rising fear. She turned her back on him, making a performance out of checking the coffee and sorting out mugs, sugar and milk. However, her hands began to shake and in despair she pressed them down hard against the countertop, finally giving voice to her anxiety.

'I know you hate me, Lucas, and you have every right to. I'm so sorry. I always knew I shouldn't have done it. Of course you want to pay me back for that… Only…' She faltered to a halt on a dry sob, biting down hard on her lip to stop her emotions getting away from her.

'Only what, Sofie?' Lucas prompted from across the room, but when she failed to answer he walked round the table, took her by the shoulders and turned her around to face him. 'Only what, Sofie?' he repeated tersely, his fingers tightening unconsciously as he saw the glitter of tears in her eyes.

'Please don't take Tom away from me. I'm begging you, Lucas. It would kill me if you did. I love him so much!' she sobbed as the tears welled up and tracked rivers down her ashen cheeks.

She didn't see the shock that swept over his face, nor the grim look that followed it. 'For God's sake, Sofie! What kind of an unfeeling monster do you think I am?' he charged, giving her a short sharp shake. 'Do you really think I would tear a five-year-old child out of his mother's arms out of sheer spite?'

Sofie stared up at him blindly, her face crumpling into lines of pure anguish. 'Some men would!'

Lucas's expression turned stony and he drew in a long breath. 'Yes, some would, but I am not like them,' he declared coldly. 'If I decide to apply for sole custody of Tom, it will be because I believe he will be better off with me, not because his mother lied to me. As it happens, I haven't made up my mind.'

Sofie drew in a ragged breath, trying to control her fears. 'You haven't? But you're thinking about it?' she queried gruffly, still shaking like a leaf.

'Of course I am. Surely you didn't think I would give up my rights without a word?' he challenged mockingly. 'I want my son, and I intend to have him. One way or another.'

She bit her lip at his words. 'What about me?' she prompted, and he made a scornful sound.

'What about you? You've had five years already. Don't you think it should be my turn?'

Her heart quailed as she listened. 'You can't do that!' she protested, and he smiled bleakly.

'I can. The question you have to ask yourself is will I,' he told her and pulled out a chair from the table. 'Sit down. I'll make us coffee.'

Sofie sat because she didn't have the strength to stand any longer. Her mind was whirling madly, so that she could barely think. 'What can I do to persuade you not to take Tom?' she asked anxiously, watching him nimbly set about pouring out two mugs of coffee.

Lucas set a mug of coffee before her. 'What, throwing yourself on my tender mercies, *caro?*' he goaded, making her wince.

Wide-eyed, she watched him pull out a chair and sit down opposite her with his own mug of steaming liquid. 'What can I do?'

He shrugged, eyes glinting scornfully. 'Depends on how far you're prepared to go,' he retorted dryly.

She swallowed hard, her answer never in doubt. 'I'd do anything.'

Taking a careful sip of the hot liquid, he looked at her over the rim of the mug. 'Anything? That's quite a tempting offer. I'll have to think if there's anything you can do that I would want,' he returned sardonically.

Sofie lowered her head, cradling the mug between her hands. 'Wh-what if I were to…reconsider my decision?' she said in a painfully tight voice.

Sitting back, Lucas stretched out his legs. 'Reconsider your decision?' he queried, as if he had no idea what she was talking about. It brought her head up immediately.

'You know what I mean!' she snapped, and he smiled.

'Yes, I know. I also know it means you're desperate.'

That was too much for her ragged nerves. 'Of course I'm desperate. I love my son!'

He sat up. 'And I have a son I want the chance to get to love!'

She stared at him, knowing she had only herself to blame for the situation she found herself in. 'I told you I won't deny you access,' she said shakily, and he shook his head.

'How decent of you to throw me a crumb. Unfortunately, if you thought I would be satisfied with that, you're much mistaken,' Lucas responded, draining his mug and pushing it aside. 'However, I shall take your offer of "anything" under advisement.'

Sofie opened her mouth to say something, then closed it again, the words unsaid. She felt helpless. Totally at his mercy. Yet a spark of spirit made her lift her head. 'Are you enjoying yourself?'

One eyebrow quirked. 'What do you think?' he charged, but she didn't bother answering. 'When can I meet him?'

Sofie drew in a shaky breath and struggled to remain calm. It was useless to try and get him to tell her his intentions. He would do that when he was good and ready. Having anticipated his wish to meet Tom, she had made plans of her own. 'He'll be home soon. Jenny's picking him up, together with her son. I was thinking that you might like to stay and have dinner with us. Tom asked for pasta tonight.'

Lucas appeared surprised yet pleased by the invitation. 'Thank you. I would like that.'

A small silence fell between them and Sofie hastened to fill it. 'He's a lovely boy. So sweet-natured and generous. He has your eyes, and mouth, and even your smile!' she told him breathlessly, smiling a little as she thought of her…their child.

One eyebrow quirked her way. 'Didn't that bother you? The fact of him looking so like me?' he asked curiously, and she shrugged.

'Not at all. I liked it,' she admitted diffidently.

That made both brows lift. 'Liked being reminded of

sleeping with a man who might be capable of doing anything to make a buck?'

Her eyes shot to link with his as she was reminded of her wild suggestions. The need to put the record straight was compelling. 'Lucas, about last night…what I said. It wasn't true.'

A mocking smile curled his lips at her claim. 'What part? You said a lot of things, as I recall.'

Sofie sighed and licked her lips nervously. 'I didn't mean any of what I said about your family's way of doing business. I only said that because I didn't want you to find out about Tom. I thought it would make you go away,' she confessed, eyes quartering his face to see if she could read what he was feeling, but his expression was closed.

'It very nearly worked. If Tom hadn't been sick, I would have been back in London right now,' he remarked coolly, and she winced.

'You have to understand. I was desperate.'

Now some emotion showed, but it was irony and gave her no comfort. 'You still are. Look at it from my point of view. You've lied so much, *caro,* how am I to know what's true or not? Once I would have trusted you implicitly, but those days are gone. However, I do believe you would say and do anything in order not to lose your son. You just as good as told me you'd sleep with me now, if that was part of the price I demanded.'

'I meant it,' she said stoically and took a long draught of coffee to bolster her nerve. She had to keep thinking of Tom.

'You wouldn't see it as a form of prostitution?' he jibed, and she flushed yet kept her chin raised.

'How could it be? We're still married,' she was quick to point out.

'So that could turn out to be fortuitous for you after all. It would certainly save your pride,' Lucas goaded softly, bringing a soft pink burn to her cheeks.

'Stop playing games, Lucas! You have the upper hand here. You know I'm at your mercy!' It sounded melodramatic even to her own ears, and yet it was exactly how things were. He held all the cards.

Her words brought a smile to his face at last. 'At my mercy. I like the sound of that. It rolls off the tongue with a certain…'

A surge of anger rose inside her at his mockery and she cut him off. 'I might have to play by your rules now, but don't for one minute think that means I'll conform to your every whim!' she warned him snappily, finishing her coffee and setting the mug aside with a decided thud.

He looked at her steadily. 'You will, or you'll lose Tom,' he declared softly, and she blanched.

Licking her lips nervously, she stared at him. 'So that's your price, is it?'

'Perhaps,' he admitted with a careless shrug. 'I'm still working out the finer points.'

Realising that she was allowing him to push her buttons far too easily, Sofie took a calming breath before responding. 'I think we should change the subject,' she suggested firmly and Lucas's smile turned more taunting even though he nodded his agreement.

'Fine by me. Why don't you tell me about your family instead? Did they know where you were? Did they know about Tom?'

It was a valid question, but she knew he wasn't going to like the answer. 'Yes. I made them promise not to tell you,' she confessed raggedly, her heartbeat raising its tempo again.

To her surprise, Lucas looked resigned, not angry. 'Well, they're your parents, so naturally they would do as you ask.

They're very loyal and never said a word,' he responded with a deep sigh.

'You're in touch?' Sofie asked, completely shaken because she had had no idea.

Lucas looked wryly amused. 'I pop in most weeks. You had no idea, did you?'

She shook her head. 'They never mentioned seeing you,' she explained, and realised that they had kept quiet so as not to hurt her. Thinking about it now, she was glad they had continued to welcome him, despite the questions in their minds. She had never told them why she had left and they hadn't asked, leaving it up to her to talk when she was ready. However, she had remained silent during their few visits and frequent telephone calls, for the hurt went too deep to talk about. After their first few attempts to get her to tell Lucas about Tom, they had given up trying as she had been adamant. They must have felt torn and she was sorry she had put them in that position.

'As I said, they keep their secrets well. Obviously they didn't think you would like to know they were seeing me.'

'I didn't think you would bother,' she said honestly, her voice barely a croak.

Lucas sat up straighter before he answered. 'Not bother? I like them. I consider them part of my family. Why should that surprise you?'

Sofie dragged a hand through her hair and sighed. 'I just never gave it a thought,' she answered, which was true enough. She had been too busy coping with morning sickness and life without him. Rising and taking their empty mugs to the sink, she was just washing them out when she heard a car approaching. Seconds later car doors slammed and childish voices piped up, calling out to each other as if they were miles away instead of a few feet. She glanced at Lucas, suddenly feeling nervous. 'Tom's back,' she told him, though he had to have guessed from the noise.

Leaving him in the kitchen, she hurried through to open the front door. Tom was just running up the front path and Sofie smiled at the state of him. He always left home neat and tidy, but returned as if he had been dragged through a hedge backwards. He caught sight of her and sped up.

'Mummy! Mummy! I got a gold star!' he exclaimed proudly and flung himself into her arms as she squatted to greet him.

Before he could squirm out of the way, she gave him a hug and a kiss. 'That's my clever boy,' she declared equally proudly, ruffling his hair. 'Did you have a good day?'

'Yep,' Tom confirmed, then she saw his eyes travel to look behind her and his head tipped as he stared over her left shoulder.

Knowing that Lucas had followed her out, Sofie slowly rose to her feet and turned, bringing Tom to stand before her, where she placed her hands gently on his shoulders. 'Tom, darling, I have a wonderful surprise for you. This is your father and he's come a long way just to see you. Be a good boy and say hello.'

Tom stared up at his father through eyes as big as saucers. 'Hello,' he said cautiously, clearly not sure how he felt, and Lucas came and squatted down before him, a gentle smile on his face.

He made no move to touch his son, merely held out his hand towards him. 'Hello, Tom. I'm pleased to meet you at last,' he declared huskily, and Sofie could hear the emotion in his voice. It made her chin wobble and brought the sting of tears to her eyes.

After a moment's hesitation, Tom reached out and placed his hand in his father's much larger one and they solemnly shook hands.

Taking his hand back, Tom's face scrunched into a frown. 'Are you really my daddy?'

'I really am,' Lucas confirmed, and Tom's frown deepened.

'Then why don't you live with us?' he demanded to know, getting right to the point as children had an unnerving habit of doing.

Amusement danced in Lucas's blue eyes as he answered the question. 'I wanted to, but things didn't turn out the way I planned. However, that's going to change now,' he added, and Tom's eyes lit up.

'You're going to live with us?' he asked excitedly, not at all bothered by the missing years. Now was far more important to him.

'We haven't quite sorted out the details yet,' Lucas admitted ruefully, glancing up at Sofie. 'Have we, Mummy?' He threw the ball into her court and she drew in a shaky breath.

'We're going to discuss it later, darling. That's why Daddy's having dinner with us,' she explained, giving Lucas a despairing look, for he had cleverly used the moment to enforce his control of the situation and she could not argue back with Tom looking on.

Tom was oblivious to the undercurrent. He was jumping up and down with delight. 'Neat!' he exclaimed, before looking questioningly at his father. 'We're having pasta. Pasta's my favourite. Is it your favourite too?' he wanted to know, and Lucas nodded solemnly.

'You know something, Tom, it is. I could eat it till it's coming out my ears,' he confessed, and Tom giggled.

Sofie looked on as father and son made an almost instant bond. Jealousy knocked on the door and she knew it was to be expected, having had Tom to herself all these years. Yet her heart was pleased to see them getting on so well from the start.

Tom was too young to have recriminations, and Lucas would never let his anger at being kept from his son show to the boy.

'Tom,' she interjected softly, and he looked round instantly. 'Why don't you take your father into the garden and show him your tree-house?' she suggested, and Tom caught one of Lucas's hands in both of his and started to tug him towards the cottage.

'Tree-house?' Lucas queried as he very nearly staggered to his feet, clearly imagining a structure high off the ground.

'It's quite safe.' She hastened to set his mind at ease. 'In fact, you're more likely to hit your head than Tom is.'

'Come *on,* Daddy!' Tom said insistently and there was no time for Lucas to say more; he could only turn and accompany his son back into the cottage.

Sighing heavily, Sofie watched them go and was left feeling almost lost. So much had happened in such a short space of time, she could barely take it in. Yet she couldn't be sorry that all the hiding was over because the guilt had haunted her. Unfortunately, in place of the guilt, she now had the anxiety of wondering just what reparation Lucas was going to demand. He had let Tom believe that the three of them were going to be living together, but she had no idea what he meant.

The question of her trusting him had suddenly lost its importance in the face of the possibility of losing her son. If she had to go back to keep Tom, then she would do it. She would have no choice. What brought a lump of emotion to her throat was the knowledge that whatever love Lucas had once had for her she had killed by the manner of her leaving him. But there was no going back. Love, once lost, was gone for ever.

Giving herself a shake, she took a deep breath and braced herself for what would happen in the next few hours. Walking back into the cottage, she went through to the kitchen and was struck by the sounds of laughter floating in from the garden. Tom's giggle was interspersed with Lucas's much deeper voice and it made her smile again as she crossed over to the window and looked out.

The sight that met her eyes had her pressing her hand over her mouth to hold back the laughter. Tom's tree-house was a sturdy structure complete with safety rails, built into a low-growing tree. It was the perfect size for a little boy, but not a grown man, and it was into this that Tom was trying with all his might to shove his father—to their mutual enjoyment. Eventually an exhausted Tom gave up and collapsed on to the grass; moments later Lucas lay down beside him.

It was exactly what Sofie needed to see to raise her bruised spirits. Her heart swelled to see the two people she loved enjoying each other's company. Laughing softly, she made up two beakers of fruit squash and carried them out into the garden. Tom took his with a bright smile and another giggle.

'Daddy was too big,' he informed her, and she chuckled.

'So I saw,' she said with a grin and held out the other beaker to Lucas, who sat up to take it with one hand and used the other to grasp her free hand.

'Join us,' he urged, tugging her down until she had to drop to her knees.

'I have the dinner to prepare,' she protested, though there was very little to do as it was a simple meal to make.

Lucas looked at her steadily, his smile hiding the steely glint in his eyes. 'I said join us,' he repeated firmly and, after meeting his look for a moment, she swallowed hard and made no further protest. 'That's better,' Lucas added with satisfaction. 'Dinner can wait. I want to enjoy watching my son, having been deprived of the novelty for so long.'

The barb found its mark with ease. 'How many times must

I apologise for that?' she asked tautly, keeping her voice low so Tom wouldn't hear.

Lucas cast her a mocking glance. 'As many times as I deem necessary. Five years is a long time.'

Sofie smiled at Tom, who grinned back, but her heart was heavy. 'And I must pay for every one of them?'

'Hour by hour. Minute by minute,' he confirmed harshly, watching their son scramble to his feet and climb inside the tree-house for a comic he had left there.

Knowing she had brought this on herself didn't make it easier to bear. 'Maybe you won't find revenge as sweet as you expect it to be,' she pointed out tersely, but he shrugged.

'It's a risk I'm prepared to take,' he declared, then drained his beaker of squash and shook out the drips before looking at her. 'You're going to have to change your name. Talbot will have to go,' he told her, and she braced herself for the first of his demands.

'Why?'

Before answering, Lucas glanced round to make sure Tom was safely out of earshot. 'Because I meant what I said to Tom. The three of us are going to be a family from this point on, and that family will have only one name—Antonetti.'

CHAPTER SIX

IT WAS to be several hours before Lucas enlarged on that bald statement. Tom had jumped back out of his tree-house at that point and joined them on the lawn, so all serious conversation had to be put to one side. Then Sofie had returned to the cottage to start preparing dinner, leaving Lucas and Tom with their heads close together, discussing things only boys would be interested in.

Dinner had always been a special time for Sofie and Tom, whilst they talked about the things they had done that day. With Lucas there, an extra dimension was added. Tom, clearly impressed by the father he had finally met, and not in the least shy, tried to copy him in everything he did, and that tugged at Sofie's heartstrings many times whilst they ate. Yet behind her relaxed attitude, her heart was fluttering anxiously. She wanted to know what else Lucas had planned and the wait was driving her crazy.

Later they returned to the sitting room, where Tom insisted on showing his father his favourite toys. Lucas appeared to have endless patience and interest, making Sofie feel guilty yet again for keeping them apart. She knew that Lucas would have enjoyed watching his son grow up. It didn't really matter if he ever forgave her for it or not, because the fact of the matter was, she would never forgive herself.

Time passed and she was only reminded of how late it was when Tom gave an enormous yawn. Glancing at the clock, she realised with a start that it was past his bedtime.

'Come along, sweetie. Time for bed. You've got school in the morning,' she told him, getting up and holding out her hand.

Tom pulled a reluctant face, yet obediently climbed off his father's lap. 'OK,' he muttered grumpily, then looked at Lucas hopefully. 'Will you put me to bed?'

Lucas glanced from his small pleading face to Sofie's expressionless one and ruffled Tom's hair. 'Not tonight, son. I think your mother would like to do that. Another time. That's a promise.'

'Will I see you in the morning?' Tom wanted to know next, and both his parents realised he expected his father to vanish as suddenly as he had appeared.

'Don't worry, Tom, I'm not going anywhere without you or your mother again. I have to work, but I'll see you after school. I'm your family now, too.'

Tom was almost convinced. 'You promise?' he insisted and, smiling, Lucas drew a cross over his heart.

'Cross my heart,' he confirmed. 'Now run along with your mother. Goodnight, son.'

Taking his mother's hand, Tom gave another big yawn. ''night, Daddy,' he returned and made no further protest but happily climbed the stairs.

It took Sofie less than half an hour to get Tom washed, dressed and into bed. The excitement of the day had worn him out and she had hardly read much of his chosen story to him when she realised he was already asleep. Tidying up his scattered clothes, she kissed him gently, switched off the light and left the door ajar. Finally she was ready to go down and face Lucas.

He was sitting where she had left him, glancing through

one of Tom's comics, but he tossed it on to the coffee table
when she walked in. He took one look at her set face and
raised an eyebrow.

'You have a problem?' he asked sardonically, which did
little to improve her mood.

Sitting at the end of the sofa, she sent him a stony look. 'I
don't appreciate you telling Tom things that you haven't dis-
cussed with me,' she declared tightly. It was bad enough that
she had no control over what happened now, without him
using their son against her.

The exact opposite to her, Lucas leaned back and looked
perfectly relaxed. 'Really? Is that a fact? Well I didn't appreciate having been kept in ignorance of my own son's existence. If you don't like my putting my son before you, too bad.
He needed the reassurance, so I told him what he needed to
hear. Do you have a problem with that?' he demanded and
Sofie sighed helplessly.

'No, of course not,' she admitted raggedly because she
would have done the same thing, except she didn't know his
plans for their future. Taking a breath to settle her shattered
nerves, she asked the all important question. 'What have you
decided to do?'

A hint of steel entered his amazing blue eyes. 'I've decided that we will be a family because I have no intention
of being a part-time father. I missed the first five years of
his life, but I'm not about to miss the rest, *caro*. Make no
mistake, Sofie, I intend to take an active part in his day-to-
day life.'

Her heart leapt a little as she heard those words. 'So you're
not going to sue for sole custody?' She sought clarification of
that most vital point. It felt to Sofie as if her whole life hung
upon the answer.

'Not yet. Whether I do or not at some time in the future depends on you. I promised Tom we were going to become a family, and that's what will happen,' he declared firmly.

Sofie blinked at him, her thoughts a blur. 'But…why? You don't even like me any more, let alone love me!' she pointed out, and a silly part of her heart was hoping he would deny her words and say he did love her. It didn't happen.

'No, I don't, but I do love my grandmother,' Lucas returned bluntly, taking her breath away for more than one reason.

'Your grandmother?' she queried faintly, completely knocked sideways. What did she have to do with this? 'I don't understand. Does she live with you?'

'No, she lives in the south of France,' he explained and, to her further surprise, dragged a hand through his hair in a gesture that revealed a hidden anxiety. 'She lost my grandfather several months ago and is not coping at all well. Nothing I, or my parents have tried has pulled her out of the depths of misery she lives in constantly. I was getting to the end of my tether when I found you and Tom.' At that point he broke off and looked at her, for once revealing the worry he felt. 'Tom could be the answer. What better than a new great-grandson to make her want to live again?'

A lump of emotion rose into Sofie's throat, as she knew exactly what he meant. Having Tom had lightened the burden of her own despair at leaving Lucas. He had been the shining light in her life—a reason to get up in the morning and look ahead with hope.

Because of that, it was the most natural thing in the world for her to reach out and touch his hand. 'I'm so sorry. You must have felt his loss deeply too,' she said softly, with ready sympathy, and felt his fingers close around hers for one vital second before he suddenly became conscious of what he was doing and released her hand, sitting back to put more distance between them.

'You don't have to start acting the part of a loving wife,' he returned ironically, and she pulled her hand back.

'I wasn't acting. Believe it or not, I can sympathise with grief, even yours!'

A nerve pulsed in his jaw. 'Maybe you can, but save it for somebody who wants it!'

Sofie bit her lip and tried not to feel hurt by this further rejection. OK, if he didn't want her sympathy she'd keep it to herself in future. She would concentrate on his grandmother instead. 'Does your grandmother have nobody else?'

Lucas shook his head. 'Only my parents and myself—and now you and Tom, of course. Which is why I'm making arrangements for us to fly out to Nice and visit her for an extended holiday. The school holidays start in a few days, which will give us enough time to get everything done.'

Impotent anger bubbled up inside her at the way he was organising her life. 'You've thought of everything, haven't you? But what about me and my life here?'

'It's over. If you want to keep Tom, your place is with me. Now, you can do this the easy way or the hard way. Try to fight me, and I promise you you'll lose.' He spelled it out to her in no uncertain terms.

Sofie gritted her teeth, knowing full well that she was trapped. 'You're taking my agreement for granted?'

Lucas's response was to smile mockingly. 'Naturally. You owe me, remember. More now than before. You will do this because you have no choice. Now, *caro,* do you really want to do it the hard way?'

She stared at him, feeling the walls closing in around her. She was helpless, and they both knew it. 'No.'

He spread his hands as if to ask what all the fuss was about. 'Then it's settled. We go to Nice. Look on it as our first family holiday together. That shouldn't be so hard to do.'

'Tom will be over the moon,' she managed to say by way of agreement, even though the words almost stuck in her throat.

'But not you,' he queried sarcastically.

'Does it matter how I feel?' she couldn't help but ask, somewhat caustically.

'I'm sure Tom would be upset if he didn't think you were happy about this,' Lucas pointed out curtly, and Sofie took a steadying breath before biting the bullet.

'Don't worry. I make a point of ensuring Tom never sees me anything other than happy and smiling. It wouldn't have been fair to offload my worries on to him,' she informed him tightly.

Lucas's blue eyes bored into hers. 'I would never doubt that you're a good mother, *caro,* but the big question now is—will you be able to pretend you love me?'

Sofie's lips parted on a tiny gasp of shock. 'Why would I have to? Tom is only five. He'll just assume we do.'

'True, but my grandmother will want proof.' Lucas dropped the bombshell with precision, knocking the breath out of her.

It was one thing to agree to go to Nice for a family holiday to help his grandmother, but to expect her to act as if they loved each other for her benefit was something else. 'You can't be serious!'

Lucas regarded her steadily. 'I've never been more so.'

Sofie shook her head to clear it. 'I can appreciate the need to help your grandmother, but why the big act?'

'Because she wants me to be happy, and when I rang her and told her that I'd found you again, and that everything was going to be all right, I could hear the change in her voice. She perked up for the first time in months.'

Sofie was flabbergasted. 'You told her that last night? Before you'd even asked me?'

He raised one eyebrow mockingly. 'We both know there was only one answer you would give, so don't sound so aggrieved, *caro*.'

Knowing he was right didn't make her feel any better. She jumped up from the sofa and paced away from him, rubbing her arms nervously. 'It's all very well for you to say all this is going to happen, but how on earth do you expect me to walk into your grandmother's house and act as if I love you?' Of course, she knew it wasn't a role she was going to have to act. She did love him, but he was putting it to the test right now!

Lucas's response turned the rack another notch. 'It shouldn't be difficult. You've done it before very convincingly. *I* actually believed you. It was a salutary lesson to discover how easy I was to fool,' he said abruptly, and her heart ached all over again.

Sofie turned back to him, feeling wretched. 'I was good, was I?' she asked in a gravelly voice, and he smiled wryly.

'The best. Which is why it should be no problem this time.'

She closed her eyes momentarily, feeling the hot sting of tears. The irony of it was that she was going to have to make it seem like an act when it was anything but, in order to protect herself. Shrugging, she pulled a face.

'It will be a hard act to follow, but I'll do my best,' she responded far more lightly than she felt. 'What other decisions have you made?' she went on, sure that there was more. She wasn't mistaken.

'I'll arrange for all your personal belongings to be packed up and delivered to our house in Hampstead whilst we're away. Tom will love it. If you remember, the garden has several trees suitable for tree-houses.'

'Thank you,' she retorted sarcastically, feeling as if she had been run over by a steamroller. 'You've been…very thorough.'

'I've tried to be. I'm having my PA look into schools in the area, although, the summer holidays are about to start. We need to get Tom's name down at a good one.'

Sofie didn't have the energy to protest. 'You see this relationship lasting some considerable time, then?' she wanted to know, and Lucas smiled.

'I consider it to be permanent. You're my wife. Tom is my son. What is more natural than for us all to be together?'

In an ideal world, of course, that would be the answer, but this was as far from ideal as it was possible to get. He didn't love her and to resume a relationship where she knew that would be soul-destroying. It occurred to her to wonder just what else was expected of her.

'I see. The marriage will be back on and I have to act as if it's for real. Do you mind telling me just how real it's going to be?'

Her question drew a sardonic look from Lucas. 'I'm sure you'll be relieved to know it will be a marriage in name only. As you said, I no longer love you, and your actions in keeping my son from me have frozen whatever attraction you had for me,' he informed her bluntly. 'I realise that a woman has needs, but you'll just have to curb them. There will be no other men, is that understood?' he added, sending a wave of shock through her system.

Loving him as she did, it had never occurred to her to take a lover. However, having him tell her she must not finally roused her anger. He had taken a lover before and it had driven her to leave him. Was she supposed to grin and bear it now? 'Does that apply to you, too? Or is there to be a double standard here?' she jibed scornfully.

Lucas's expression grew stony. 'What I do is my business. What I expect of my wife is another matter.'

'I see,' she responded tightly, having her answer. She must be above suspicion, whilst he could do as he liked because there was nothing she could do about it. Not if she wanted to keep Tom.

Lucas's eyes were gleaming, for he could read the impotent anger raging inside her. 'You can always say no.'

Sofie would dearly love to be able to throw his demands back in his face, but knew she didn't dare. She was in an unenviable position and had no other option but to agree to everything.

'I have no choice but to accept those terms and you know it,' she told him shortly and drew in a sharp breath when she saw satisfaction flit across his face for a second. 'I'll make some coffee,' she declared brusquely, turning abruptly and bustling into the kitchen before he could say anything else.

Once there, though, she made no attempt to make the promised drink, but instead walked to the sink and stood staring out of the window. She was devastated and her heart shredded with the knowledge of what was expected of her. An empty shell of a marriage to a man she actually loved was so far from what she wanted her heart wept. Except it wasn't her feelings she had to worry about. This was about Tom. Giving their son a normal family life. Surely the lack of love for herself would be nothing compared to what Tom would get out of it. She wanted Tom to know his father and, searching her heart, she knew she loved them both enough to put her feelings aside.

Yet that didn't stop her being angry at Lucas's double standard. She didn't want any other lover but him, but that was beside the point. His declaration that he could do as he pleased told her she had been right to leave him. He had destroyed her trust and would have no compunction about doing so again. Only this time she had to stay. She had to be strong, for Tom's sake. More than that, she had to be strong for herself, and never let him see just how much she still loved him. If she could do that, then she could keep her pride intact.

Her happiness would come from seeing Tom happy and flourishing.

With that settled in her mind, Sofie found a sort of peace. She took a steadying breath and briskly set about making the coffee. Carrying the two steaming mugs into the sitting room, she set one before Lucas and cradled the other between her hands on her lap.

'You were gone a long time,' he pointed out, frowning, as if he could sense a subtle change in her, yet couldn't work out why.

'I was thinking. Considering my options—or lack of them,' she responded tiredly. 'I had no idea you could be so ruthless.'

'I'm not, as a rule, but you drove me to it. Blame yourself if you don't like the result,' Lucas advised, watching her over his mug as he sipped his coffee.

She frowned at him. 'If you despise me so much, why insist I come back?'

'That's for Tom. He needs you. I don't,' Lucas replied bluntly, and the words stung as they were meant to do.

'How will you bear having to see me every day? Won't that just rub salt into the wound?' she jibed, trying to hit back, but it bounced off him without leaving a mark.

'I'm prepared to make sacrifices for Tom's sake,' he retorted, and she saw red.

'How very noble!'

Lucas set his mug down and leant towards her. 'Be careful how you talk to me, *caro*. I don't have to do anything I don't want to, whilst you will have nothing unless I agree to it. Tread softly, or take the consequences.'

Her heart quailed at the very real threat and she swallowed nervously. 'And if I don't?' she challenged him and went cold when she saw the steel in his eyes.

'Then losing Tom becomes a very real possibility.'

They stared at each other, but in the end she was forced to look away. 'Damn you,' she muttered softly, but he heard.

'You damned me, *caro,* when you ran away. Now, let's get everything settled. It's getting late,' he declared with finality. 'I plan on flying out to Nice the first week of the holidays. Do you have a passport for Tom?'

'Yes,' she confirmed, struggling to keep her tone free of all emotion.

Lucas raised an eyebrow. 'What name did you use?' he asked.

'Antonetti. I didn't want to have to explain the different names,' she revealed, and wasn't surprised to see the sardonic gleam in his eye.

'So it was convenient to be my wife sometimes?' he drawled mockingly, and Sofie grimaced but remained silent.

'OK, I'll go ahead and book the tickets. Now, I'd better get moving,' he went on, rising effortlessly to his feet. 'I'll be busy most of the day, but I will be back before Tom gets out of school.'

Sofie let his assumption that this would be OK pass by. If this was the way things were to be, the sooner she got used to it the better. She had to keep her eyes on the prize, and the prize was Tom. 'You'll stay for dinner. Tom will expect it,' she told him, rising too and heading towards the front door.

'I shall be looking forward to it. I had forgotten how good a cook you are, *caro,*' he complimented her, and Sofie had to admit she was surprised.

Which was why she turned round to look at him instead of looking where she was going. 'I would have thought the food would stick in your throat,' she retorted wryly, but there was no chance for Lucas to respond because at that precise moment she inadvertently trod on one of Tom's abandoned roller skates and her foot went out from under her.

Uttering a strangled cry of alarm, she began to fall backwards, arms cartwheeling in a vain attempt to save herself. However, she had no need to fear, as her fall was halted midway by a strong pair of arms closing round her. Suddenly she found herself hauled up and into the safety of Lucas's chest as if she weighed nothing at all.

In the second it took to get her breath back, she was very much aware of the warmth and scent of him and her senses responded accordingly, bringing her body to life. Needs suppressed out of necessity rose to the surface, bringing with it the remembered ache of desire. Pressed against him, she could hear his heart beating, the rhythm matching her own, which was racing, as much from the shock of her near fall as finding herself once more in his arms. Her lips parted in wonder and it was the most natural thing to tip back her head and look up at him.

Lucas was staring down at her and she knew she had taken him by surprise because there was just enough time to catch the heat and hunger in his eyes before he muttered something unintelligible and brought his mouth down on hers.

His kiss was as hot and hungry as that brief look in his eyes and, unable to help herself, Sofie welcomed it like the warming rays of the sun after an endless chill. Passionately demanding, it left no room for thought, only feeling. Too wild to last long, it left her gasping for breath and longing for more when Lucas finally dragged his mouth away from hers. Then he looked at her bruised lips and flushed cheeks as if surprised to see her there. In an instant he had set her back on her feet and stepped away.

'That wasn't supposed to happen,' he declared abruptly. 'It won't be happening again, either, so you can stop those little tricks, *caro*. I meant what I said—I'm no longer interested.' With that he walked to the front door and let himself out, pausing only briefly to glance back at her. 'Until tomorrow,' he added, then was gone.

Sofie stared after him in bemusement, gently pressing her fingers to her kiss-bruised lips. For a man who had twice declared his lack of interest, that had been a very passionate kiss! She knew better than to read any finer emotions into it but, as to him feeling nothing, that was a lie. He was protesting too much. She knew how difficult it was to stop wanting someone. It wasn't like switching a light on and off. Maybe he didn't want to want her, now that he knew about Tom, but that was a different thing altogether.

Bending down, she picked up the roller skate and held it tightly in her hands. If the wanting was still there, then maybe, just maybe, there was a chance of rekindling the passion. She bit her lip and her heart skipped at the thought of herself and Lucas becoming lovers once more. She couldn't hope for love, for the way she had hurt him had hardened his heart, but perhaps she could have him in her arms again. Know the taste, scent and feel of him. Yet did she want that? The answer was swift and sure. Oh, yes. She craved it. She wanted to feel warm again. Alive again. Only Lucas could do that.

She caught back a sob as tiredness overcame her. Lucas was everything to her and it really didn't matter if she trusted him or not now. She had to do what he wanted in order to keep her beloved Tom. She was trapped but there was a faint glimmer of hope that her situation might not be as arid as she had expected. Passion without love was a poor substitute, but it was all she could hope for. Yet, if it happened, she wasn't going to start believing everything was going to be all right because she dared not trust him. To do so would leave her open and vulnerable, so she had to harden her heart, take what she could, and hope and pray it was enough for the long years ahead.

CHAPTER SEVEN

THEY flew to the south of France at the end of July. Lucas had stayed up north for a week, visiting Tom every day and forging a bond that had become unbreakable in no time at all. He had been friendly towards Sofie, but she was very much aware that a barrier had gone up. He had kept his distance without ever appearing to do so to their son. When he had had to go back to London to work he had phoned Tom every evening, chatting about this and that, whilst his conversations with herself had been businesslike. Well, they had not even been conversations. He had told her what he wanted her to do and she had to agree.

Tom was ecstatic about going to live with his father and had just as much enthusiasm about their holiday. Sofie listened to all the things he wanted to do with an aching heart. She would remember it all at the end of the day, after she'd put him to bed, and would laugh and cry at the same time. She had never given a hint of her misgivings. So far as Tom was concerned, she was as delighted about everything as he was.

Lucas had booked them into first class and that was as much a novelty for Sofie as it was for Tom, who had never flown before. He had the window seat so he could look out and watch the world go by below them. However, not long after lunch the excitement took its toll and he fell asleep.

'Does your grandmother know we're coming today?' Sofie asked as Lucas sat down after angling Tom's seat backwards so he could sleep more comfortably.

'Of course. I couldn't have the three of us descend on her unannounced,' Lucas answered and she asked the question she had been holding back for days.

'How did she take it?'

'With a great deal of pleasure,' he said, then quirked an eyebrow at her. 'Are you worried about meeting her?'

'How much does she know about us?' she asked uneasily, thinking how it had occurred to her that she might not be too welcome in his grandmother's house. She had the vague memory of meeting her at the wedding, but they hadn't spoken for very long.

Lucas laughed mockingly. 'Don't worry, I didn't tell her that you left me because my money wasn't quite the draw you thought it was. Or that the sex was great, but living with me wasn't. I told her we had had a foolish argument, which had kept us apart too long. We've now patched things up and have decided we want to live together as a family.'

Sofie licked her lips nervously, knowing it wasn't going to be that simple. 'She believed you?'

'As to that, I couldn't say.' He shrugged. 'We'll find out soon enough.'

That was true, she admitted to herself, glancing down at her fingers, which had a tendency to fidget nervously these days. 'Did you see my parents whilst you were home?' she asked, looking up.

Lucas stared at her for a moment, his expression sardonic.

'I did,' he returned, but didn't expand that further, clearly leaving her to do the questioning.

Sofie drew in a long breath, wondering when his need to punish her would end. OK, they would do it the hard way. 'How were they?'

'They're in the best of health and over the moon to hear that we are getting back together again. They were a little surprised that you hadn't rung to tell them yourself, but I explained how busy you were, getting ready for the move,' he reported casually and Sofie could feel the heat rise in her cheeks. 'Why didn't you tell them, *caro?* Too much of a coward?'

That immediately roused her temper and she shot him a glare. 'What did you expect me to say? Oh, by the way, I saw Lucas the other day and, guess what, he's blackmailing me into going back to him,' she snapped in a sibilant undertone and Lucas laughed harshly.

'Telling the truth would be breaking the habit of a lifetime,' he responded bluntly and the look he gave her was heavy with irony. 'All you had to do was make up another lie,' he went on provokingly and she ground her teeth together in impotent anger.

'When it comes to lying, you're pretty good at it yourself,' she retorted gruffly. Of course, she was referring to his actions which had destroyed her trust and sent her running away from him in the first place. Lucas, however, was thinking of the present.

'White lies hurt nobody. It's the bald-faced black ones that destroy,' he returned forcefully, blue eyes boring into hers.

She stared at him, breath caught in her throat. 'Are you saying I destroyed you?'

He shook his head, lips curving into a grim smile. 'I didn't let you. Instead, I decided that one day I would have my revenge for the way you walked out on me.'

Swallowing hard, she looked deep into his eyes, but saw only herself reflected there. 'Be careful, Lucas. Revenge can often destroy the one seeking it,' she warned him.

He raised an eyebrow mockingly. 'Worried for my soul, *caro*? Or just worried for yourself?'

'Myself, obviously. Isn't that what you expect me to say?' she replied, managing to find the necessary amount of mockery to hide behind, and turned away from him to check on Tom.

She was reaching over, brushing a stray strand of hair off Tom's cheek, when she felt Lucas take her left hand. She looked back at once, to see him frowning. 'What is it?'

'Damn, I forgot to get you a ring,' he explained, patently annoyed with himself. 'My grandmother will notice that right away. She has eyes like a hawk.'

Sofie's heart gave an odd lurch and she eased her hand free as she reached down for her bag. 'Don't worry,' she reassured him, searching the zip pocket inside for a chamois encased package. She unwrapped it to reveal her diamond wedding band. She hadn't brought it with her intending to wear it, but because she couldn't leave it behind. It always had and always would go everywhere with her.

Lucas picked it up and his surprise was evident in his tone. 'You kept it? Now you really have astonished me. I thought you would have got rid of it long since,' he murmured, looking at her curiously.

There was no way she could tell him she would never part with it, so she shrugged in an offhand way. 'You know what they say about diamonds. It was always there if I needed it.'

He found that totally believable and his lips twisted into a wry smile. 'A girl's best friend, no less? And there was I thinking you might have kept it for sentimental reasons.'

Sofie gave him an old-fashioned look. 'Why would I do

that?' she asked, and he laughed, picking up her hand and slipping the ring back on to her marriage finger.

'Why indeed? There, you're now official again.'

She stared at the ring, which still fitted perfectly, and couldn't withhold the surge of emotion which welled up inside her. There had been such hope on the day he had first set it on her finger, but this time there was none. 'What about your ring?' she asked, attempting to divert the swell of emotion inside her, and he held up his left hand.

'I never took it off. What kind of a fool does that make me? No, don't bother to answer. We both know. Anyway, the rings are merely dressing. What you have to do is convince my grandmother that you're madly in love with me still.'

Sofie took her hand back with feigned amusement, hiding the fact that her heart had just squeezed painfully. 'I don't know if I can do madly in love just like that,' she remarked jokingly. Which was a downright lie, for it was the only thing she did know how to do, being the simple truth of her feelings for him.

'Just do what you did before, *amore*. No doubt it will all come back to you. Like riding a bike, you never forget,' he returned sardonically, and she drew in a pained breath.

'You know, this can't all be one-sided. You have to do your part too,' she reminded him sharply and he smiled mockingly.

'Don't worry, I'll manage to hide my distaste well enough to convince my grandmother,' he informed her bluntly and, because that stung, she had to hit back.

'Strange, I don't remember you kissing me with distaste the other night. That came after, when you implied you regretted it,' she retorted smoothly, and he looked at her with his eyes narrowed.

'There was nothing implied about it,' he declared forcefully, and she allowed a tiny smile to hover about her lips to show she wasn't convinced.

'OK, if you say so.' She shrugged and for once quite enjoyed seeing his face tighten with annoyance.

'I do say so. Don't start with your tricks. I won't be falling for them this time,' Lucas cautioned and she cast him a look from the corner of her eye.

'I get the message. There's no need to belabour the point or I might think you're protesting too much!' she goaded lightly and her ears delighted to the sound of a sharply indrawn breath.

'Cut it out, Sofie,' he growled and, smiling to herself, she abandoned her taunts and reached for the headphones so she could watch a movie. Not that she concentrated much at first as her thoughts were still on Lucas. It felt good not to let him have it all his own way. Let him think she was playing games—that way he would never guess that what he saw were her true feelings and not the act he expected her to put on for the sake of his grandmother. After all, she needed to protect herself, too.

Nice Airport was bathed in glorious sunshine as they came in to land. Everything was going smoothly until they came out of Customs and then they found themselves caught up in a great uproar. Suddenly flashlights were going off all over the place and Sofie realised they were caught up in the entourage of a celebrity footballer. Tom, standing within feet of one of his heros, was in seventh heaven. For his parents it was another matter. With nowhere to go, they had to wait for the way to clear, and it was during this time that Sofie noted that English newspapers and TV were fully represented. She jotted down the relevant names, hoping that she might be able to buy a copy of a photo with Tom and the footballer in it. He would be the envy of all his friends.

Eventually Lucas managed to get the three of them, plus luggage, over to one side, out of the glare of publicity. 'They're moving off now. Let's go and pick up the car I arranged for and get out of this madhouse.'

Sofie laughed at his disgusted expression. 'Don't you like football?' she teased him and, for the first time in for ever, he looked at her with real humour.

'Football, yes. Flashbulbs blinding me, no!'

She chuckled and they grinned at each other, sharing a rare moment of empathy.

Sofie grabbed the memory and stored it in her heart, where all her happy memories lived, then returned to the more mundane task of getting out of the airport. Once they were safely in the car and heading out along the coast road, however, she began to feel nervousness build inside her again. It was one thing to be compelled to do as Lucas asked, but quite another to put into practice. How could his grandmother be happy to see her, knowing what she had done? The woman didn't need to know the details to be protective of her grandson. She would be angry on his behalf, and that did not bode well for their relationship.

Fortunately there were spectacular views as they drove along the coast and Sofie was distracted by the sheer beauty of that part of the country. She wished she had thought to put a camera in her bag, but they were packed away in her cases. The road twisted and turned, sometimes rising to giddy heights, and it was as they began to descend again that Lucas pointed out a red-tiled roof a little ahead and below them.

'That's the villa.'

'Wow!' Tom exclaimed in awed tones, his nose pressed against the window.

Though she didn't say it, Sofie echoed his thoughts. The villa sprawled out below them, with gardens to one side and a sparkling blue swimming pool to the other.

'It's beautiful, but isn't it a bit big for your grandmother?' Sofie felt compelled to ask as Lucas steered the car round some very sharp bends, then in through a pair of iron gates and down the drive to stop by the garage.

'Physically, yes, but it's crammed to the gills with memories, so she will never part with it. Now, though, she has the prospect of family visits to fill the rooms with laughter again,' Lucas explained as he switched off the engine and climbed out.

Their son could certainly sound like a herd of elephants, Sofie thought whimsically as she followed suit. Tom had already jumped out of the back and was running along the path.

'I bet it's got a hundred bedrooms!' he exclaimed, grinning at his father, who had followed him.

Lucas laughed and ruffled his hair. 'Not quite that many.'

'Which one's mine?' Tom wanted to know next, jigging from one foot to the other, a sign Sofie recognised immediately.

'Yours will be round the back. You'll see it in a minute,' Lucas replied.

'The bedroom can wait,' Sofie pronounced decisively, joining them. 'Right now Tom needs the toilet.'

'There's one through the hall. Come with me, son.' Lucas held out a hand, which Tom took, and the pair of them swiftly disappeared into the building.

Sofie slowly wandered inside after them, glancing around her with real pleasure. The understated elegance of the villa struck her immediately. Someone had a real eye for decoration.

'Hello, there!' a gentle voice exclaimed from behind her. 'We meet again, Sofie.'

Spinning round, Sofie saw a shadowy figure standing in the doorway. She stepped forwards into the hall, and Sofie was finally able to see the elderly elegant woman, carrying a basket of flowers. Her smile was reserved, whilst her eyes were haunted, as a sign of her recent grief.

Sofie immediately felt the ever-present guilt she suffered from rise to the surface as she faced Lucas's grandmother for the first time since the wedding. Warmth staining her cheeks, she took a step towards the older woman.

Drawing on all her courage, she held out her hand. 'How do you do, Mrs Antonetti? I'm pleased to meet you once more. Er... Lucas won't be a moment. He's taken Tom to the bathroom,' she explained, her smile coming and going under a forthright stare.

There was only the briefest flicker of hesitation before Eleanor Antonetti took Sofie's hand and kissed her on both cheeks. 'Please, call me Nell. Two Mrs Antonettis in the house will be too confusing,' she explained, looking her grandson's wife over and seeming to like what she saw.

'I was just admiring your home,' Sofie went on conversationally and Eleanor Antonetti glanced around her with simple pride.

'Why, thank you, my dear. We worked hard on it for many years, getting it just the way we wanted it. My husband and I were very happy here. I was just picking some flowers for the lounge when I heard you arrive.' She indicated her basket, which she set down on a side table. 'Marco loved lilies,' she added with a sigh, then made a visible effort not to get maudlin. 'Tom is your little boy, my great-grandson?'

Sofie smiled, as she always did when speaking of Tom. 'Yes. He can be a bit boisterous, I'm afraid.'

'Good,' Eleanor declared with satisfaction. 'This place needs laughter again. Ah, that sounds like him now.'

On cue, Lucas, with an excited Tom in tow, re-entered the hall. Tom ran to Sofie, whilst Lucas greeted his grandmother with a warm hug.

'You're looking better, darling. There's colour in your cheeks again. How do you feel?'

Eleanor patted his arm as he released her. 'I'm fine. Don't fuss. Sofie and I have been getting reacquainted. And this must be Tom…' she declared, getting her first good look at him standing before Sofie. She gasped audibly, her hands going up to her cheeks as she registered the likeness between father and son. 'My goodness! He's the image of you, Lucas!'

Sofie bent down to her son's ear. 'Go and say hello to your great-grandmother, Tom,' she urged him, giving him a gentle push forwards.

Tom shuffled forwards with all the awkwardness of a child towards an adult he didn't know. 'Hello,' he said, frowning heavily, glancing back at Sofie, who nodded encouragingly.

Eleanor bent down towards him and smiled. 'Hello, Tom. What a big boy you are! Would you mind very much giving an old lady a hug?'

Tom shook his head solemnly. 'I don't mind,' he said brightly. 'I like old ladies,' he added and in the next second folded his little arms around her neck.

Sofie wasn't sure how Eleanor Antonetti reacted, because her own eyes were awash with tears. Oh, how she loved that little boy! When she was able to see again, Eleanor had Tom's cheeks framed with her hands and was pressing a kiss to his forehead.

'Ah, Tom, Tom. You're a sight for sore eyes!' she exclaimed, straightening up.

Tom blinked up at her. 'Do they hurt? Did somebody hit them?'

'What, dear?' his great-grandmother asked, puzzled.

'Your eyes. You said they were sore,' Tom explained, and Eleanor chuckled delightedly.

'No, dear. It's just something we say when we see someone we like. Are you thirsty, Tom? I bet we can find something cold for you in the kitchen. Why don't you come along with me and we'll check it out?'

'That went off remarkably well,' Lucas observed, coming to stand beside Sofie as his grandmother and son went away together in search of cold drinks. 'I can see already that he will be good for her.'

Sofie sniffed and wiped her eyes on a tissue she'd found in her pocket. 'I'm sure you're right,' she agreed. 'Your grandmother was very kind to me.'

Lucas looked at her, eyebrows raised. 'What did you expect?'

'She would have been well within her rights to be cool. After all, I was the one who walked out,' she reminded him.

'True,' Lucas conceded, 'but that's all behind us now. We simply have to prove to her that it was all a silly misunderstanding and that we're happy to be together.'

Sofie let out a long breath, pulling a face. 'That's a big ask.'

'But not beyond your abilities. We both know what you're capable of. You could do this blindfolded,' he returned with heavy irony, but Sofie shook her head.

'I'm no actress,' she argued and he caught her chin in his fingers, raising her head until she was looking into his eyes.

'On the contrary, you are a consummate actress. Your acting in the past deserved an Oscar. Just do what you do best and lie your head off. Tell her what you know she needs to hear, just like you did with me. You'll have her convinced in no time at all!'

Sofie stared up at him, hot tears burning the backs of her eyes, knowing that she had not been playing a part. Her feelings had been honest and true. Unlike his. 'You go too far!' she protested thickly, forcing the words out.

His expression turned steely. 'But you'll take it, because of Tom,' he told her coldly, and she let out a ragged breath.

'You never used to be so cold!'

Lucas smiled mockingly. 'No, I learned that the hard way, from you. Now, pull yourself together before my grandmother comes looking for us. Take my arm,' he ordered and, when she hesitated, held it out. 'Do it, *caro*. Don't forget what you could lose.'

His reminder was unnecessary. She knew full well. Squaring her shoulders, she slipped her arm through his. 'OK, I'm ready. Is this all right, or should I look a bit more besotted?' she enquired dulcetly, batting her eyes at him, whilst inside her heart was weeping.

Lucas smiled wryly. 'Don't overdo it,' he warned her.

'You can't overdo madly in love. It's an all or nothing feeling,' she reminded him, dropping the adoring look. She couldn't have kept it up anyway.

'I'll bow to your superior acting skills,' he shot back sardonically, and Sofie winced inwardly. He never lost an opportunity to shoot her down.

'That wasn't very lover-like,' she reprimanded him, but he merely shrugged. 'You have a part to play too.'

'When the moment requires it, I'll do my bit,' he assured her, and she sighed heavily.

'I could do with a drink.'

'A large brandy would go down a treat, but it looks like all that's on offer is lemonade,' he said tersely. 'Come on, let's do this before my nerve runs out.'

Her eyebrows shot up. 'When did you ever get nervous?' she asked, and he gave her a look.

'On our wedding day. I imagined you not turning up. Which is laughable now, when you consider how things turned out.'

He had never told her that before and it turned her heart over. She, on the other hand, had been supremely confident on their wedding day. Certain that this was the right thing to do and that their love for each other would get them through their life together. She had believed him to be a man to be trusted, but ultimately he had let her down. Now she knew that she couldn't trust any man. Not that it mattered. Lucas didn't want her love or her trust. He wanted Tom and she was just part of the package.

However, she wasn't going to think about that now. She had a job to do and she had to do it well, so as not to risk losing her son.

She was very much aware of Eleanor Antonetti giving them both a quick searching look when they walked into the kitchen. So his grandmother wasn't quite as credulous as he thought. It would make her task that much harder, but she knew she could do it. After all, she really did love Lucas. The only acting she was doing was pretending to him it was all an act.

They all sat out on the terrace, with spectacular views of the sea, and drank deliciously cold glasses of homemade lemonade. Eventually Tom started to get antsy, as small boys did, and Lucas took him off to show him the wonders of the garden, leaving Sofie alone with his grandmother.

They sat in comfortable silence for a while, but finally Eleanor spoke.

'When my grandson visited here after you had left him, I was shocked. I had never seen him so distraught. I hope never to see him that way again,' she said in her gentle voice and turned to look directly into Sofie's eyes. '*Do* you love him?' she asked and Sofie's heart leapt at the direct question.

However, she had no trouble answering it with absolute honesty. 'With all my heart. I always will, no matter what happens.'

Eleanor raised a questioning eyebrow. 'Do you expect something to happen?'

Sofie was annoyed at herself for making the slip. She was supposed to be confident, not doubtful. 'You have to know better than anyone that things don't always turn out as planned, Mrs Antonetti…Nell.'

The older woman nodded wisely. 'Ah, you're referring to my husband. I wish we could have had more time together, but what we did have was a joy. He was the perfect husband, perfect father. I have many happy memories.'

How Sofie wished that she could say the same thing about her own marriage. The happiness had faded fast in the face of Lucas's betrayal. He had pulled the rug out from under her feet and left her with nothing to hold on to. Her love hadn't been enough. It had only made her more vulnerable. How could she believe that anything he had said and done was real?

A soft touch on her arm made her jump and she realised she had been lost in her own thoughts for a few minutes. One look at Eleanor Antonetti showed she was frowning with mild concern.

'Are you all right, Sofie? You looked quite sad for a moment. Is there something you want to talk about?'

Sofie immediately shook her head and produced a bright smile. 'It's nothing. Really. Where do you think Lucas and Tom have got to?' she said changing the subject swiftly. Whilst the other woman let it go, had Sofie been looking at her, she would have seen that she was not about to forget the last few minutes.

'The swimming pool, probably. Let's go find them, shall we? I can show you my garden at the same time,' Eleanor suggested, and Sofie was quick to fall in with it, for the conversation had become too close for comfort.

They took a leisurely stroll through the garden and indeed found father and son sitting by the swimming pool. They spent the rest of the afternoon there, until it was time to freshen up for dinner. Then Sofie took Tom to his room, which she was amazed to see full of every toy and gadget a young boy could ask for. After she had given him a quick wash, she left him playing with some of the toys whilst she went to the bedroom she was to share with Lucas.

He was inside when she walked in, stripped to the waist as he prepared to change his shirt. He looked up as she closed the door. 'Tom OK?' he asked, and Sofie nodded whilst the thinking part of her brain shut down and the sensual one took control.

'He's playing,' she reported, her voice getting croaky as she admired the tanned planes of Lucas's powerful chest. She hadn't seen him other than fully clothed since she had left him six years ago, and the urge to go to him and run her hands over the torso she had once been so familiar with was immensely strong. Her palms tingled and she curled her hands into fists at her sides. 'Your grandmother must have raided the local toy store.'

Lucas chuckled. 'As she didn't know what he's into, she probably got a bit of everything. Don't forget, she's got five years of birthdays and Christmases to make up for.'

The sound of his laughter turned her heart over and she took a shaky breath as she started to walk towards him. 'He'll get spoilt.'

'Doubtless, but that's what grandparents do best,' he agreed, glancing at his wrist-watch. 'You'd better get a move on. Gina unpacked for you,' he added as he turned back to the bed where he had laid out his clean shirt.

Sofie couldn't seem to take her eyes off all the tanned flesh that rippled as he moved. It was a magnet that drew her and it suddenly occurred to her that there wasn't anything to stop her from doing exactly what she wanted to do—touch him. He wanted her to act the part of a woman in love, and what would such a woman do when she encountered her man only partially dressed?

Had she not been pretending to pretend, she probably wouldn't have done it but, because she was, she allowed a wicked imp of mischief to take control and reached out to place the palms of her hands on him. 'Mmm,' she sighed sensually. 'You feel good.'

Lucas didn't exactly jump, but he straightened up at once and the tension in him was palpable. 'What the hell are you doing?' he growled, and there was something in his tone which made her smile. He wasn't immune.

'Touching you,' she replied huskily. 'I'm madly in love, remember. If you're going to walk around our room half naked, you can't expect me to keep my hands to myself,' she enlarged on the theme, and gently drew her nails down his spine. 'Do you like that?'

She knew he did from his swift intake of breath, and touching him was certainly raising her own temperature. Very softly, she pressed her lips to the silky smooth flesh and breathed in the heady scent of him. Her eyelids dropped down and, without thinking, her arms slid around his waist, her hands rising to find his broad chest.

Immediately Lucas's hands grasped her wrists and pulled

her hands away. 'OK, that's enough!' he ordered sharply, making enough room for himself so that he could turn to face her. A nerve pulsed in Lucas's jaw as he stared at her. 'I'm sure you've discovered a whole load of fancy tricks in the years we were apart, but I don't want you practising them on me!'

The claim stung and brought her head up. 'Is that so? You know something, Lucas Antonetti, you're a liar! I was getting a totally different message!' she fired back and was pleased to see his jaw clench in reaction. At which time she moved away from him and made a production out of yawning and stretching. 'Besides, there's no need to get all hot and bothered; I was just practising. Getting my role right,' she taunted, opening a couple of drawers until she found the top she was looking for, then faced him again. 'How did I do?'

Lucas was watching her like a hawk and just knowing that did her a power of good. At least he wasn't ignoring her. 'Trust me,' he said at last. 'You don't need any practice.'

That brought a saucy smile to her lips. 'Now that's what a woman likes to hear,' she flirted and slipped into the connecting bathroom before he could form a reply.

Leaning back against the door, she pressed her hands over her thundering heart. Mercy, that had been an interesting few minutes. Even if Lucas wasn't hot and bothered, she was. The thought entered her head that she needed a cold shower and that made her laugh and groan. Maybe it hadn't been the wisest thing to do, but she wasn't sorry because she had learned a lot. Lucas didn't hold all the cards. When it came to the attraction he still felt for her she had the power to undermine his resolve. Not that he would make it easy. If she wanted them to make love, she would have to try and seduce him. So the big question now was, did she want to try it or not? Would it make things better or worse? She honestly did not know and it was easier to push it to the back of her mind and concentrate instead on washing and changing her clothes.

Dinner was a light-hearted affair and much laughter rippled around the table set on the patio to catch the warm evening breezes. Lucas was so relaxed that it was easy for Sofie to put all her troubles behind her temporarily and simply enjoy the moment. Eleanor had a wealth of stories to tell about her grandson, and she had Tom giggling with the tales of his father's exploits.

'Of course, your daddy had to do all these things on his own, Tom,' she told him confidentially. 'However, I'm sure Mummy and Daddy plan to give you a little brother or sister to play with. Maybe even two or three,' she added, giving Lucas and Sofie an appealing smile.

'We haven't even thought about it yet,' Lucas responded and his grandmother tutted.

'Well, you should. You're not getting any younger, you know.'

'Thank you for pointing that out,' he said sardonically. 'Excuse me whilst I go and apply for my bus pass!'

Sofie laughed and, momentarily secure in the role she was playing, reached over and squeezed his hand. 'Never mind, darling, I'll still love you when you're all old and wrinkly,' she teased lightly, her heart lurching when he raised his eyebrows at her audacity. 'I would love a daughter. Boys are great, but you can't dress them in pretty clothes like you can a girl. Two would be even better, then a boy to even things up. How does that sound?'

'It sounds like you're going to be kept busy, Lucas,' Eleanor put in with a gurgling laugh.

Something twinkled in Lucas's eyes and he surprised Sofie

by raising her hand to his lips and kissing it. 'I think this is something we should discuss in private,' he said huskily, squeezing her fingers just a little more than was necessary. Sofie hid her wince behind a soft laugh.

'Oh, but I remember you once saying you wanted half a dozen children, at least…darling,' she responded in a saccharine tone, pulling her hand free.

Tom stared at them both and pulled a sickly face. 'Ugh… That means kissing stuff!' he said disgustedly, and they all laughed.

Lucas reached across the table and ruffled his hair. 'When you're older, you'll find kissing stuff isn't so bad.'

'Not me!' Tom denied strongly. 'Melanie Nicholls kissed me at school and it was all sloppy! I don't want girls kissing me like that!'

'Take my word for it, son,' Lucas said seriously. 'Not all girls kiss like Melanie Nicholls. Now, your mother here, she's a good kisser,' he added, giving Sofie a wicked look out of the corner of his eye.

Tom's jaw dropped as he looked at his mother, seeing her in a whole new light. 'She is?'

'Sure she is! Don't you like it when she gives you a hug and a kiss?'

'Uh-hum,' the little boy agreed happily, grinning at his mother and looking so much like his father that it squeezed her heart. 'I like Mummy kissing me.'

Sofie smiled at him, all the love she felt glowing in her eyes. 'That's good, darling, because I like kissing you, too!'

'Do you like kissing Daddy?' he asked in the next breath, causing his great-grandmother to catch her breath, and his mother's heart to tweak yet again.

'As a matter of fact, Tom, I do. Now, I think you'd better

eat up. It won't be long until bedtime,' she reminded him in a tone he knew well.

Conversation turned to more mundane topics for the rest of the meal. An hour later, Sofie took an exhausted Tom up to bed, where he was asleep before his head touched the pillow. Smiling gently, she tucked him up, pressed a kiss to his forehead, then went back to join the others.

Lucas and Eleanor were still sitting at the table, drinking coffee, but when Sofie went to sit down Lucas caught her hand as she passed. She looked at him questioningly.

'Walk with me,' he invited. 'It's a lovely evening and the views are quite spectacular at night.'

'Yes, do,' his grandmother encouraged. 'It's very romantic,' she added with a twinkling smile.

Sofie smiled back. 'Romantic? Sounds good to me.'

'I'll keep an ear out for Tom, don't worry,' Eleanor promised as Lucas stood up, still keeping hold of Sofie's hand.

'Don't wait up. We may be some time,' he told his grandmother, who laughed and waved them off.

They wandered along the terrace and down the steps into the very Italianate gardens of the villa. Everything was lush and a riot of colour and scents. It was highly romantic and extremely relaxing.

'So,' Lucas declared after a short while had passed, 'you like kissing me, do you?'

Sofie's heart leapt into her throat at the question. She knew she could lie, but what was the point? He had to know. 'You're very good at it.'

'Hmm, you were pretty hot yourself. The sex was always good between us. It was a shame you couldn't live with the rest of it,' he said dryly, and Sofie sighed.

'Why go raking over old ground? I'm here now, doing

what you want,' she pointed out tiredly. 'You could try cutting me some slack, you know.' Much to her surprise, he didn't come back with a sharp remark, but merely sighed.

'That doesn't come easy, *caro*.'

Her laugh was almost defeated. 'Why? I'm not going anywhere. If I want my son, I have to stay wherever you are. You know I could never leave him, so I have to do as you want. If that means pretending to your grandmother that we love each other, so be it. I'll do anything so long as you don't take my son away from me. I'm here to stay.'

Lucas came to a halt and turned her to face him. 'You said you loved me, but you left anyway,' he reminded her in a gentler tone than he had used before.

She shook her head despairingly. 'That was different. I…just had to go. I couldn't leave Tom. It would kill me.' She looked into his eyes, trying to read what he was thinking. 'It would destroy me. Is that what you want? Would that be enough to satisfy your thirst for revenge?'

Lucas dragged a hand through his hair and swore softly. 'I thought so once. Now… Now I'm not so sure. I want to keep hating you, but this damn thing between us keeps getting in the way! Why did you have to touch me earlier?'

'What?' she gasped, flung totally off balance by the question. Looking at him now, it was as if he had raised a barrier, for suddenly she could see a fierce emotion gleaming in his eyes.

'I've been doing my damnedest to keep you at arm's length, but you had to go and test me, didn't you, *caro?* You had to go and rock the boat!'

Her eyes widened as she struggled to take in what he was saying. 'No!' she denied, but he smiled tautly.

'Yes. You did. Damn you, *caro,* you know I want you so

much it's like knives tearing me apart!' he declared with a passion that took her breath away.

Sofie blinked up at him, her heart thundering wildly in her chest. 'But you said you didn't want me,' she stammered. Even though she hadn't believed it, his almost angry confession was staggering.

'I lied,' he gritted out, releasing her shoulders and walking on a few steps. Then he looked back. 'I took a leaf out of your book and lied.'

'Lied?' she repeated, knowing she sounded like an idiot, but unable to get her brain working properly. 'Why?'

Lucas shook his head and laughed. 'Because I was angry. After I found out about Tom, I no longer had to get you in my bed for revenge, I had other ways to go about it. But you've always known I still want you, despite what I said.'

Suddenly realising she might not have to seduce him after all, Sofie gathered her scattered wits and folded her arms. 'Do I?' she asked, striving to sound cool.

'Don't act coy, *caro*. You more or less told me so only a couple of hours ago.'

Which, being true, she could hardly deny. 'Yet it's a reluctant wanting, isn't it? You'd much rather not feel that way.'

Lucas shrugged. 'What sane man would want to admit that he's still attracted to the woman who walked out on him? Who withheld the fact that he was a father from him? Well, I've admitted it, which means I must be crazy, because there's something about you, *caro*, that pulls me to you in spite of myself. I know you've lied to me. I suspect you will probably do so in the future, but it doesn't stop me wanting you. My need outweighs my better judgement. Isn't that what you've been waiting to hear?'

Sofie glanced away, staring out over the bay but seeing

nothing of it. Despite the loss of trust his betrayal had caused, her heart still wanted to hear that he loved her. How stupid was that? But this wasn't about love or trust, it was as basic as it could get. They were talking about desire. About the longing for each other that had refused to go away. It would never be enough, but it would be something.

In the moonlight, she could see the wicked gleam that entered his eyes. 'There's nothing stopping you touching me now,' he invited huskily, and her heart skipped a beat.

'Out here?'

'Why not?' he challenged, closing the gap between them until it was barely there. 'Backing out, *caro?*' he goaded.

Sofie shook her head, glancing back towards the villa where she could see Eleanor sitting at the table. 'No, but your grandmother can see us.'

A roguish smile curved his lips and he reached out to place his hands on her hips and urge her forward. 'All the better, then. We want her to know how happy we are. So…whenever you're ready…'

Oh, he reckoned he was so smart, Sofie thought to herself. He was leaving it up to her, and no doubt believed she would chicken out, given their audience, but she was braver than that. Placing her palms flat against his shirt, and immediately feeling the warmth of his body, she looked up at him teasingly.

'Are you sure you want me to do this?' she queried, sliding her palms upwards until they slipped into the open neck of his shirt and stroked firm male flesh.

Lucas's response was to pull her hips tight against his. 'I'm game if you are,' he growled, setting her senses alight in no time at all.

'OK,' she murmured softly and, framing his head with her hands, began to plant a tantalising row of kisses along the line of his jaw until she reached his chin, then she changed her line of attack to his beautifully shaped mouth.

It was highly arousing to hear his intake of breath when her teeth gently nipped at his bottom lip, and the catch in his throat when her tongue flickered over the very same spot. Laughing softly, she angled her head, the better to tease him with lips and tongue, delighting in his response but refusing to deepen the kiss. In the end it was Lucas who was compelled to stop her sensual forays by holding her head still. Only then did she accept the invitation he offered and took his mouth, their tongues engaging in a sensual dance that heated her blood and started a fire low down inside her.

By this time both had forgotten their audience and, as kiss followed kiss, each more hotly erotic than the last, desire mounted between them until it was like a volcano poised on the edge of eruption. They drew apart finally, only because of a need to breathe, and then it was mere inches. Their heated breath mingled as they looked at each other.

'I'd forgotten how wild an adventure kissing you could be,' Lucas confessed raggedly.

'I tried to warn you,' Sofie couldn't resist telling him, though her own actions had rebounded on her.

Lucas managed a wry smile. 'So you did,' he agreed, his voice husky with passion.

'Do you think we convinced your grandmother?' Sofie asked next and they both looked to the place they had last seen her. The table was empty.

'She's gone in,' Lucas observed. 'Probably didn't want to play voyeur. Things were beginning to get a little torrid.'

'We ought to go inside. Your grandmother was probably embarrassed,' Sofie proposed, feeling more than a little embarrassed herself.

'She didn't come down in the last shower of rain, *caro*. However, you're right, we should go in. I have a phone call to make,' Lucas responded soberly.

Sofie was about to answer when they both heard a muffled sound. 'That's Tom!' she exclaimed, recognising the sound of his crying. 'He must have woken up and not known where he is!' she added, freeing herself from his arms and heading for the path up to the villa.

Lucas followed at her heels and they were almost there when Eleanor Antonetti came out of the house.

'Tom's awake. He wants you, Sofie,' she explained immediately, and Sofie realised Eleanor must have heard him earlier, whilst they had been otherwise engaged, and deaf to everything around them. Colour swept up into her cheeks.

'I must go to him. Excuse me,' she said and, without looking either of them in the face, disappeared inside.

Eleanor turned to her grandson. 'Interesting. I wouldn't imagine the woman you talked about all those years ago would be able to blush.'

Lucas nodded his head slowly. 'No, you wouldn't,' he agreed with a frown. 'Sometimes she's like an open book, and at others I can't read her at all.'

His grandmother laughed. 'In fact, just like a woman,' she pointed out wisely, and he sighed ruefully.

'Do you mind if I use the study? I have some business to do. Seeing as my wife is otherwise occupied, I might as well get on with it,' he decided, and stooped to kiss her cheek. 'Goodnight. I'll see you in the morning,' he added, and disappeared, too.

It was almost an hour before Lucas finished what turned out to be a series of telephone calls and went off in search of his wife. When she wasn't in their bedroom, he backtracked to Tom's room.

The sight that met his eyes brought him to a halt in the doorway. Tom was now asleep again, sprawled across the bed like an exhausted cherub, whilst Sofie sat in a chair beside him, fast asleep. Quietly he crossed the room and picked her up, freezing when she made a snuffling sound, but when she didn't wake he carried her out of the room and back to their own bed. There he carefully laid her down and removed everything save her underwear and pulled the sheet up over her.

For a moment he stood looking down at her, wishing he could penetrate the wall of her mind and see what was going on there. Knowing he couldn't, he sighed and took himself off to the bathroom to shower. Sofie hadn't moved an inch when he returned and he abandoned the towel he had wrapped around his hips before slipping into the bed beside her. Before too long they were both asleep.

CHAPTER EIGHT

SOFIE sighed softly and stretched like a cat. At which point she discovered her pillow was gently rising and falling. For one nanosecond she was startled, but then her senses woke up and she recognised the male scent she breathed in. Lucas. Quickly following that knowledge, she realised her cheek was resting on his chest and one of her legs was curled around one of his. Not only that, but his left arm was anchoring her to his side, one large hand resting on her hip.

Without opening her eyes, Sofie attempted to work out how she had got in such a position and could only imagine that she must have rolled over in her sleep and coiled herself around him. In the few months they had been together six years ago, they had slept this way most nights, and in her sleep she had instinctively sought out that source of comfort and safety.

She smiled to herself, enjoying the rare moment. She was going to savour every second before Lucas woke up and the world impinged itself on them again. Slowly, slowly, she began to explore the silken flesh beneath her fingers, gliding over his powerful chest and flat abdomen, finally coming to a fluttery halt over his bare hip.

One thought shot to her brain. Lucas was naked. Another

thought followed. It felt like she was, too! Now it wasn't that she had anything against two consenting adults being naked in a bed, but she did find it alarming that she had no recollection of getting there—or what had happened after that!

At the precise moment she was having these startled thoughts, she heard the tempo of Lucas's heartbeat change. She registered he must be awake just as he spoke.

'Why did you stop? It was just beginning to get interesting,' he asked in a sexy growl and her heart skipped a beat.

Sofie opened her eyes at last and tipped her head up so she could see his face. Lucas was looking down at her with stubble on his chin and mayhem in his wicked blue eyes.

'You have no clothes on,' she pointed out, wincing at how prudish that sounded. Lucas must have thought so, too, for he grinned.

'I always sleep with nothing on. You knew that, or have you forgotten, *caro*? You started to sleep that way, too.'

'I know I did, but why am I that way now? What happened last night?'

'Ah,' Lucas uttered knowingly, and laughed softly. 'So that's the way of it, is it? You don't remember.'

Her nerves skittered. 'What don't I remember?'

'*Caro,* you were incredible. A revelation. So wildly passionate you took my breath away,' he told her fervently. 'How could you have forgotten?'

She almost fell for it until she saw his lips twitch as he tried not to grin. 'You're making it up! Nothing happened, did it?'

He shrugged. 'Only in my dreams,' he admitted, and she frowned.

'Then how come I have nothing on?' she demanded to know.

'Because, when I carried you to bed, I undressed you. For modesty's sake, I left your underwear on.' To prove it, Lucas caught the lacy elastic at her hip and snapped it. 'Not that it hid much, hence my dreams.'

'You could have woken me, so I could change,' she argued, finally recalling what had happened in the garden last night.

Lucas had stopped fighting his desire for her. They would probably have made love last night had Tom not woken up. She remembered settling him down again, and sitting in the chair beside him. That was where she must have fallen asleep. Then Lucas had found her and brought her back here and put her to bed.

'I could,' he agreed, lazily running a finger up her arm to her shoulder, then down again to the swell of her breast. 'However, you were more in need of sleep than a nightie, so I left you dreaming like a baby.'

Right now, lying so closely next to him, and with his finger exploring dangerously close to the front fastening of her bra, she didn't feel in the least like a baby. Drawing in a shaky breath, she licked her lips. 'Well, I'm awake now,' she reminded him huskily, and his smile grew sultry.

'Hmm, just in time for a good-morning kiss,' he murmured, shifting slightly so that he could bring his mouth down on hers.

As good morning kisses went, it worked wonders, stimulating her system, bringing her senses to life and sending her blood pulsing through her veins. She made a low catlike growl in her throat and raised her hand to slip her fingers into his hair and keep him where he was.

Meanwhile, Lucas's fingers had not stopped their exploration. With ease he snapped open the fastening of her bra and pushed the silky scraps of material aside to cup her breast in his hand. Sofie gasped as her nipple engorged, pressing into his palm, making her instinctively arch herself closer. His touch was gentle, but the stroking of his thumb across the hardened tip was scintillatingly erotic. In response she deepened the kiss, slipping her tongue into his mouth to engage with his, joining in a mating dance as old as time.

When Lucas finally dragged his mouth from hers, they were both breathing heavily and Sofie lay back, looking up at him through misty eyes. Smiling, Lucas turned his gaze to where his hand still held her breast captive.

'There's more of you than there used to be,' he observed thickly, lowering his head to tease her nipple with his lips, which stole her breath away and deepened the throbbing ache which had started deep inside her.

Sofie had to struggle to concentrate in order to reply because he was working magic that made thought impossible. 'I had a baby, remember,' she said, gasping again as his tongue licked her sensitised flesh. Automatically her fingers clenched in his hair and her eyelids fluttered down.

'Mmm, all the more for me to hold,' he responded as he removed her bra completely and tossed it aside. Then he transferred his attention to her other breast and Sofie arched her back to offer herself more fully to his exquisite ministrations.

He was driving her mad, teasing and caressing by turns, and all the while the coils of desire began to tighten and spiral upwards. It had been so long since he'd touched her, and she was so needy she knew it wouldn't take much to send her over the edge. As if he sensed it, Lucas ended his ravishment of her breasts and raised his head to watch as he stroked his hand down over her hip and across the slight mound of her stomach. A faint silvery line caught his eye and he traced it with his finger before looking at her.

'What's this?' he asked curiously, and Sofie opened her eyes again.

'A stretch mark. I have a couple that didn't go. Do you mind?'

Enlightened, he gently ran his hand over her stomach. 'Not at all. They're the proud marks of motherhood, reminding me how you bore our son. Because of that, they will always be beautiful to me. *You* are beautiful to me, *caro*,' he told her earnestly, holding her gaze so that she would know he didn't lie.

She shook her head slightly as moisture dazzled her eyes and her heart turned over. 'Most men wouldn't agree.'

'I'm not most men, *amore*. I am your husband, and I know what true beauty is.'

In a few words he had managed to remove any doubts she had had about the desirability of her body. 'Ah, Lucas,' she murmured with a watery sigh. She loved him so much it broke her heart to know he could never feel the same way about her.

Then she forgot all about it as Lucas began pressing a row of tiny kisses across her stomach, and turned her thoughts to jelly yet again. She barely felt him remove her panties and toss them aside, but the glide of his palms up her legs and over her thighs set her pulse racing. She reached out to touch him, but fell back with an aching moan as he pushed her thighs apart and sought out the moist, throbbing centre of her desire. His fingers teased and stroked, stoking the embers of need until they grew red-hot and her hands dug into the sheets as she fought to hold on to sanity and not plunge over the edge into the stunning freefall of release.

'No, no!' she pleaded through gritted teeth. 'Wait!' She wanted them to be together, joined, so that they could ride the roller coaster in each other's arms.

Lucas had other plans, and when his lips and tongue took over the devastating caresses she was lost. Her climax was white-hot and furious and, as she lay there waiting for her heartbeat to slow and her breathing to steady, her emotions see-sawed between enjoyment of the sheer pleasure and sadness that they hadn't made the journey together.

He must have sensed her dismay because seconds later Lucas propped himself up on his elbow beside her and cupped her cheek with his hand. When she looked at him through accusing eyes, he smiled faintly.

'Don't be angry, *caro*,' he soothed softly. 'It gave me pleasure to pleasure you.'

'And what about what I wanted?' she charged back, her voice still choked with emotion.

At the question his smile broadened and his eyes glinted wickedly. 'I cannot take it back, *caro*, but they say turnabout is fair play,' he said with a sexy growl. 'Do what you want, I won't stop you.' To underline the invitation, he lay back on the bed and waited silently.

Sofie rolled on to her front and looked at him. 'You know, that was a rash thing to say. You may come to regret it,' she warned him, whilst all sorts of possibilities were running through her mind.

He smiled lazily. 'There are many things I may regret in my life, but having you make love to me isn't one of them.'

Make love to me. The words echoed in her heart. She would be doing that in its truest sense. Giving physical expression to what she didn't dare tell him. He didn't believe she loved him, or ever had, and it was better for herself that he went on thinking that way.

So she began. Very gently, so that it was barely a touch at all, she started to smooth her hands over his chest, each caress imprinting a memory of him in her mind. Yet at the same time she remembered all the sensual tricks she had once used to arouse him, and began the task of undermining his control. The flick of her finger over one flat nipple caused a sharp intake of breath and when she used her teeth to gently bite him, then soothed the flesh with the brush of her tongue, she felt his whole body tense and he muttered something unintelligible under his breath.

Delighted with her success so far, Sofie expanded her area of exploration, delighting in the strength and breadth of his broad shoulders before seeking out his other nipple and treating it to the same delicate torture. She soon found that to use all her imagination to arouse him was in its turn arousing her. Tracing her way down his body—over his flat abdomen, then lower still—she used hands, lips and tongue in a journey of rediscovery. That her tantalising caresses were having the desired effect was visible enough when she finally reached the hardened length of his manhood.

Whilst Sofie found it highly erotic to know she could do this to him, she wanted more. She wanted him to lose control the way she had. It wouldn't take much, as she could feel the tension in him as he waited, could feel the increased thud of his heart beating in time with her own. Which was why she didn't immediately do what he expected, but straddled his legs and trailed her hands over his powerful thighs, teasing him by coming unbearably close and still avoiding that most desired contact.

Every time she came close, she could see the muscles in his stomach clenching, and she looked at him, her lips curved into a catlike smile that hid the fact that desire was once again a coiled spring inside her. Lucas had one arm over his eyes, but he raised it to look at her when she spoke.

'How am I doing so far?'

'You're enjoying this, aren't you, *caro?*' he growled at her, and she laughed softly at his predicament.

'I can stop if you like,' she offered, and his eyes glinted with the promise of mayhem.

'Do, and I won't be responsible for what would happen next!'

Sofie was tempted to stop just to find out, but her own needs were almost as strong as his, so instead she shook her head until her hair swung loose about her and trailed the silky ends of it across his heated flesh. The effect was all she could have hoped for. Lucas's hips jack-knifed off the bed and he swore violently in Italian as he drew in a hissing breath through his teeth and battled to retain control.

Not wanting that, Sofie moved until she was positioned over him and carefully lowered herself, taking him deep inside her with a soft moan of pleasure. Very slowly she began to move, wanting to drive him crazy, but discovered that her own body began to betray her. There was no way she could arouse him without arousing herself, and she bit her lip, striving to resist the demands of her own desire.

That was when Lucas took control once more. His hands rose to her breasts, moulding them, teasing her ultra-sensitive nipples, turning the embers of need into a raging furnace that refused to be denied. A whimper escaped her and her movements grew wilder until Lucas moved his hands to span her hips and hold her still.

'Wait,' he urged gutturally, his voice thick with passion, whilst his hands glided up her back, urging her down towards him. Sofie sank down until she lay against his chest. 'Together this time,' he breathed against her lips as he rolled them over until he was resting in the cradle of her thighs.

Sofie didn't care to argue. All she knew was that they were driving each other crazy and the solution lay within their control. When Lucas began to move, thrusting into her with increasing tempo, she wrapped her legs around him and matched him thrust for thrust. In minutes they were beyond the point of no return and there was only one place to go.

Their climax was so powerful they both cried out together, holding on as the delicious waves of pleasure carried them upwards to dizzying heights, and then slowly brought them back down again. For long moments all was still, the only sounds they could hear were pounding hearts and laboured breathing. Yet eventually even that ceased and they lay in each other's arms, replete at last.

More than half asleep himself, Lucas pulled the silk sheet back over them. 'Sleep now, *caro,*' he said gently, and closed his eyes as Sofie snuggled into the crook of his arm.

Sofie stirred for the second time some hours later. This time she knew where she was right away, and she wasn't lying on Lucas's chest. In fact, on opening her eyes to have a look, she discovered she was alone in the bed. Which was disappointing, but allowed her to lie back and run through all that had happened in her mind.

Their lovemaking had been unbelievable. Way beyond what she had expected. She felt like the cat who'd got the cream—full to the brim with satisfaction. It would only have been bettered if Lucas had still been here with her, but she knew better than to wish for everything. She was lucky to have what she had.

She was still thinking that when she became aware of Tom's laughter from not far away. In fact, it was getting closer all the time. He was saying something and a deeper voice was answering. Realising she was about to be invaded, she just had time to make sure the sheet covered her properly when Tom burst into the room, closely followed by Lucas.

'Mummy! Mummy!' her son chanted as he dashed for the bed and, whilst she held one hand out towards him, her eyes flew to Lucas.

Acknowledgement of what had passed between them mere hours before was in his eyes, along with something else she couldn't quite put a finger on. Then she forgot all about it when he smiled. It always had been a smile to take her breath away, but now it felt as if the wattage had increased and she basked in its warmth.

'Where did you get to? I missed you,' she told him huskily, clutching on to the sheet as Tom bounded on to the bed.

'I went to see what Tom was doing, then got him washed and dressed,' Lucas explained, sitting down on the end of the bed whilst Tom started bouncing up and down.

'Daddy's going to teach me to swim,' he announced as he went up.

'Wow! Aren't you the lucky one? Daddy's a good swimmer. In fact, Daddy's good at a lot of things,' Sofie added wryly, giving Lucas a look from beneath her lashes which made him grin.

Tom did another two bounces before expanding on his theme. 'We're going later, after my breakfast has gone down.'

Sofie kept a firm grip on the sheet, which was about to escape due to their son's bouncing. 'That's good. You don't want to get cramp,' she told him seriously, then made a grab for his hand. 'Hey, when are you going to give me a good morning kiss?'

'Right now!' he exclaimed, landing on his knees and pitching forward into her arms. Sofie collapsed with him on top of her and they exchanged several noisy kisses.

Eventually Lucas stood up again. 'Come on, Tiger. Let's get you something to eat or you'll have to wait longer to get into the pool. We'll leave Mummy to get dressed in peace.'

When they had gone, Sofie wiped away a single tear that escaped down her cheek. This was how her life should have been—could have been even now if she thought Lucas loved her, and had the courage to try trusting him again. The sad part was, her own action in leaving him had destroyed whatever he *had* felt for her, so now all that was left was the wanting. Yet she couldn't have stayed, so there was no way out of the vicious circle. All she could do was make the best of what she had. Now wasn't the time to look the gift horse in the mouth.

The thought made it possible for her to get up and shower, dress herself in shorts and a strappy top, slip her feet into sandals and go in search of the others with a calm expression on her face. She found them on the terrace, seated at the table, the remains of a substantial breakfast littering the surface.

Sofie stopped in the doorway to take in the scene. Two dark heads were tipped close to each other as Lucas listened to something Tom was whispering to him. They were so alike, her heart swelled with so much pleasure that her chin wobbled and she had to raise a hand and press it to her lips. If anything happened to either of them, she would fall apart.

Fearing that if she stayed there too long she would be discovered, Sofie took a deep steadying breath, steeled herself for the fray and stepped outside.

'Good morning. It's a lovely day,' she greeted to the table at large and three heads turned in her direction. It was Eleanor who held out a hand to her and Sofie took it, bending to kiss the older woman's cheek and receiving a similar salute in return.

'Good morning, Sofie. Did you sleep well?' Eleanor asked as her granddaughter-in-law straightened up.

'Very well, thank you,' Sofie responded, darting a glance at Lucas, who was watching her intently.

'Do I get one of those?' he asked.

'Of course,' Sofie replied, bending to kiss his cheek, but he moved his head quickly so her lips landed on his.

'I slept well, too,' he told her in a whisper as she drew back, bringing a wash of soft pink to her cheeks.

'So,' Eleanor said, once Sofie had taken a seat and the housekeeper had been asked to bring fresh warm croissants and coffee. 'Are you going to swim, too?'

Sofie shook her head. 'I think I'm going to be lazy today. But I shall go and watch.' There was no way she could let Tom take his first swimming lesson and not be there to make sure all was well. Lucas was a good swimmer but, as a mother, she had to be on hand, just in case. And cheer Tom on, of course.

The housekeeper arrived with a tray and a message for Lucas that he was wanted on the telephone. He disappeared inside the villa and didn't return until Sofie had almost finished her second cup of coffee. Eleanor had taken Tom indoors to get him into his swimming trunks and find the armbands she had bought him, leaving Sofie alone to enjoy the peace and quiet.

'Trouble?' she asked Lucas as he sat down opposite her.

'Not at all. It's an old problem that is now, thankfully, pretty much solved. You know how it is—doing the obvious thing is often the last thing you think of,' he explained. Resting his elbow on the table and his chin on his hand, he watched her with a brooding look in his eyes.

'That's good,' she replied, frowning at him as his fixed stare made her want to squirm. 'Do I have jam on my nose or something?' she asked.

'No, I'm just enjoying the view,' he returned gallantly.

'So was I until you sat in front of it,' she riposted teasingly, bringing a glint to his endlessly fascinating blue eyes.

'Not nice, *caro*. That requires some sort of payment.'

She smiled broadly. 'Uh-uh. I don't think so,' she denied, draining her cup and setting it aside. 'I think I'll see how

Tom's getting on,' she added, pushing herself to her feet, but, before she could take a step further, Lucas caught her by the arm and started to pull her round the table towards him.

'Oh, no, *caro,* you don't get away that easily!' he threatened as she did her best to resist him and tug her arm free.

'Brute! Philistine!' she lambasted him, laughing all the while.

Of course, there was no doubting how the tussle would end. Lucas was far stronger than her and, though his grip was gentle, there was no breaking it. He gave one final tug and she landed on his knees, his arms going round her to hold her captive.

'Apologise,' he commanded, his fingers seeking out the ticklish places at her waist.

'Never!' Sofie vowed, squirming as he unerringly found the most sensitive spot, making her dissolve into a fit of giggles. Twisting and turning like fury, she struggled to free herself whilst Lucas continued to tickle her mercilessly. Then, completely unintentionally, their combined movements brought his hand in contact with her breast, and they both went still.

'Well, now, isn't this cosy?' Lucas declared huskily, his eyes gleaming wickedly.

'You realise Tom and your grandmother could come back at any moment,' Sofie reminded him, trying to ignore the pleasure she was getting from the warmth of his touch.

'Then you'd better apologise quickly, hadn't you?' He grinned.

She immediately shook her head. 'Not if my life depended on it!' She refused point-blank to give in and was never more relieved to hear their son's childish treble piping up not far away.

Hearing it, too, Lucas smiled ruefully. 'Saved in the nick of time,' he said, releasing her and helping her to her feet, where she just had time to smooth her clothes and hair back into place before Eleanor and Tom emerged from the villa.

Sofie had to smile when she saw her son, for not only was he wearing a dashing pair of electric-blue trunks, but inflated armbands, too.

'Can we go yet?' he asked his father eagerly.

Nodding, Lucas rose to his feet and took Tom by the hand. 'Coming, Mummy?' he asked Sofie.

Try and stop me, she thought, taking Tom's other hand. 'Of course,' she confirmed, then glanced at Eleanor. 'Will you join us?'

'You three go ahead,' she refused with a smile. 'I have a few things to do, but I'll pop down later. Have fun!'

Fun was the operative word when they reached the pool. Tom wasn't the least bit afraid of water and would probably have jumped in at the deep end if Lucas hadn't cautioned him. Sofie's heart was beating just a little faster with natural anxiety, but that soon passed when she saw how good Lucas was with their son. He was an excellent teacher, and had the patience of a saint. It wasn't long before Tom, with the aid of his armbands, was able to do a creditable doggy-paddle from one side of the pool to the other. Of course, he made a lot of splashing along the way, almost drowning his father once with a surging bow wave.

When Lucas emerged, coughing and spluttering, Sofie burst out laughing, which drew a threatening look from her husband.

'Think that's funny, do you?' he growled and, sweeping Tom out of the water, carried him to the side and sat him down. 'Stay there,' he ordered in a voice that promised he'd be sorry if he didn't, and waded out of the pool.

Sofie watched wide-eyed as Lucas prowled towards her. He looked magnificent, with his long-legged powerful body clad in a minuscule pair of black Speedos. Her heart turned over for quite a different reason, and began racing with an emotion as far removed from anxiety as it was possible to get.

As he got closer she held up her hands to fend him off, expecting to get showered with water, but Lucas had other plans. Instead of shaking his head over her, he bent and swept her up off the sun-lounger and turned back to the pool.

Sofie gasped, realising his intent. 'Don't you dare!' she squealed, and he grinned at her.

'Bet you wish you'd apologised earlier, now,' he taunted, stopping at the edge.

She took a look at the sparkling blue water below her and clamped her arms around his neck. 'I'm sorry. I apologise,' she declared hastily, only to see his grin broaden.

'Too late, *caro*,' he said, and jumped out into the deep water.

Sofie screamed, but the water closing over her head cut it off. Lucas had let go of her as they entered the water, so when her feet touched the bottom she pushed hard and kicked her way to the surface. Soaked to the skin, she looked around for Lucas, but only saw Tom, sitting on the pool-side, laughing uproariously. She just had time to wave to him, when her ankle was caught and she was pulled down again.

Lucas swam in front of her. Grinning from ear to ear, he captured her head between his hands, pulled her forward and kissed her. It was a deeply sensual kiss, seeking a response from her which she was unable to deny him. Her arms went around him and their legs entangled, keeping them together. Highly erotic, it couldn't last long as the need for air forced them apart and they shot to the surface in a surge of splash and spray.

'Just you wait, Lucas Antonetti,' Sofie threatened, though she was laughing as she kicked away from him and swam down to where Tom, no longer laughing, waited. Finding her feet, she smiled at him reassuringly. 'OK, darling?'

'I don't like it when you go under the water,' he said heavily.

She gave him a quick hug. 'I know. Daddy was just mucking about. He only did it because he knows I can swim. He won't do it to you. Are you coming in again?' she asked, holding out her arms to help him down.

Tom brightened instantly and jumped down. 'Aren't you going to put a swimming costume on?' he wanted to know, and Sofie pulled a wry face.

'I don't think I'll bother now. Can't get any wetter, can I?'

Tom giggled and began splashing around, happy as Larry. Lucas emerged a few feet away, sweeping his hair back from his eyes, looking pleased with himself.

'You're a little overdressed, *caro.*'

Sofie gave him a narrow-eyed look. 'I'll tell you what you are, later.'

He grinned that wolfish grin that set her nerves tingling. 'I'll look forward to it,' he responded huskily, and swam over to where Tom was heading too far out of his depth.

Sighing, Sofie watched the two of them and it occurred to her that, for the first time in for ever, she was truly happy. It didn't matter that it might not last. For this one moment in time at least, everything she wanted was right here by her side where it was meant to be.

CHAPTER NINE

THE next few days were, for Sofie, like having all her Christmases come at once. They were magical, and every moment was a joy to be locked away in her heart and treasured. Lucas was once again the man she remembered, giving no sign of the anger he had felt at his discovery that he had a son. She wasn't foolish enough to think he had forgotten, but she hoped that he was on the way to forgiving as she was starting to forgive him for his betrayal.

Meanwhile Tom had flourished under the attention of three loving adults and, as Lucas had hoped, the change in Eleanor was marked. Her great-grandson had brought a joy of life back to her and, though she would mourn the loss of her husband for a long time to come, Tom was the shining light which gave her a reason to get out of bed each morning. He, in his turn, loved her, as she was not above getting down on the floor with him and playing cars.

So those were the days. The nights were a different kind of heaven. In the darkness Sofie and Lucas came together with a passion that never seemed to fade. There were moments when the beauty of their lovemaking brought her to the verge of tears. Last night had been such a night and, had she not known in her heart that Lucas did not love her, she would have been certain that he did feel something powerful.

Which was why she sighed wistfully, gently stroking the strong tanned arm which curled around her waist. They lay spoon-fashion and she liked the feel of him touching her from head to toe. It made her feel…protected, and it was foolish for her to wish that it would also make her feel loved.

She sighed again and the arm around her tightened a fraction. It was the first intimation she had that he was awake.

'You sound a little sad. What's wrong? I thought you were happy here,' Lucas asked, his voice still gravelly from sleep.

'I am,' she agreed instantly. 'This is a beautiful place, and I love your grandmother. She's such a warm, generous person. Tom adores her.'

'That's because she gives him everything he wants,' Lucas said dryly. 'She'll spoil him rotten.'

Sofie laughed. 'Yes, but you'll see his head is screwed on right,' she added with certainty and satisfaction. She twisted round so that they were facing each other. She liked seeing Lucas with faint stubble on his chin. It made him look wild and rakish. 'Did I say how sorry I was for keeping him from you?'

He smiled, magnifying the rakish effect a hundredfold. 'Yes, but you can tell me again if you like,' he invited as his hand travelled over her hip and thigh, drawing her leg up and over his so he could nestle against her.

Sofie's breath hitched in her throat as she became aware of his arousal. Her body, which had still been sluggish from sleep, immediately woke up, sending delicious tingles along her senses. 'I don't think conversation is what you want,' she told him with a sultry look from beneath her lashes.

His teeth flashed whitely as he grinned. 'There's conversation and then there's…' he rolled his hips teasingly '…conversation.'

She laughed softly, whilst her body began to pulse with re-kindled desire. 'Ah, I get it now. Actions speak louder than words,' she flirted, pressing a tantalisingly brief kiss on his lips. 'Did you know that for every action there is an equal and opposite reaction?'

'Oh, yes. It's what I'm counting on,' he growled sexily, and proceeded to take her mouth in a slow, deeply arousing kiss.

That kiss led to another, and another and, before long, they were lost to the outside world.

Later they showered and dressed and went to find Tom, but he was already having breakfast with his great-grandmother. After she had kissed him good morning, Sofie sat down and tucked into the mouth-watering food laid out on the table. She was ravenous, and it wasn't entirely due to the fresh air—a fact that hadn't gone unnoticed, she discovered, when she caught Lucas's eye and saw the wicked glint in it.

'Don't!' she warned, her eyes drawing his attention to their son. Tom was likely to ask embarrassing questions and she would rather avoid that.

Lucas's lips twitched. 'I was only going to say I like a woman with a good appetite.'

'Stop teasing the poor girl, Lucas. Just remember, little pitchers have big ears,' his grandmother cautioned him with a glance at Tom, who was steering a toy car around the pots and plates on the table whilst he ate. 'Do you have any plans for the day? You could go to the market. Tom and I will be perfectly all right here, won't we, Tom?'

He looked up with a cheeky grin. 'She's going to race cars with me. She's cool!'

Sofie laughed. 'You're a lucky boy, to have her.'

Tom looked at her seriously. 'And there's Daddy's mummy and daddy. Am I going to see them too?'

Lucas nodded. 'Of course. Probably as soon as we get home. They're looking forward to meeting you.'

'OK.' Tom accepted that with a tiny shrug and started zooming his car around again.

Sofie stared at her husband in surprise, but all he did was smile at her and ask, 'Shall we go to the market?'

Pulling herself together rapidly, Sofie nodded. 'Yes, please.'

'Have lunch out,' Eleanor urged them. 'You two need some time alone together. I'm only on the end of the phone. Make a day of it.'

'Are you trying to get rid of us?' Lucas enquired wryly, and Eleanor smiled conspiratorially.

'Tom and I have plans and we don't need you here. So shoo!' She waved her hands at him. 'Go. Have fun. Don't come back until you're worn out and weary!'

Laughing, Lucas rose to his feet. 'OK, we get the message. We won't stay where we're not wanted. Tom, you be a good boy, and maybe we'll bring you something back from the market,' he promised his son, who grinned and nodded. Then he looked at his wife. 'Are you ready?'

Sofie jumped to her feet. 'I have to get my bag. I'll meet you out by the car,' she told him, then turned to Eleanor. 'Are you sure you're OK with Tom? He can be a bit of a handful.'

'We'll be fine. Have a good day, and take all the time you need,' Eleanor responded, patting her arm.

'Thank you,' Sofie breathed as she bent to kiss the older woman's cheek. Then she ruffled Tom's hair and disappeared inside.

Ten minutes later, she and Lucas were in the car heading

down towards the coast. He drove slowly, as there was no rush. Sofie sat back in her seat and felt more relaxed than she had for a long time. With the whole day ahead of them, the world was their oyster. Or it was, until Lucas spoke.

'Why were you surprised when you learned I had let my parents know about Tom? I had to tell them some time,' he remarked as he steered the car round a series of hairpin bends.

'I know—' she sighed '—I guess I'm still thinking I have to keep him secret. And…' She hesitated over the next words, unwilling to face the answer she might get.

Lucas darted her a swift glance before returning his attention to the road. 'And?' he prompted.

Sofie pulled a wry face. 'And I didn't want to hear that they hated me for keeping Tom from them.'

'They don't hate you. They were hurt and disappointed, but that will pass. You'll have to give them time,' Lucas explained, easing the car over so another vehicle could pass them.

She had to admit it was a relief to hear him say that because she liked his parents and never wanted to hurt them. 'They'll love Tom,' she pronounced, smiling as she thought of it.

Lucas chuckled. 'I defy anyone not to love Tom. I loved him from the moment I saw him,' he declared and she looked round at him, not so much in surprise as curiosity.

'You did?'

'He's my son, *caro*. One look was all it took for him to capture my heart,' he confessed, and invisible fingers squeezed her own heart.

'That's how I felt, too. The nurse laid him in my arms and he held on to my finger as if he was never going to let go,' she said softly. Just like his father, he had found his place in her heart and soul and could never be removed. She only had to look at her feelings for Lucas to know that. He had betrayed her. Had broken her trust. Yet she still loved him. She always would.

'We're hostages to fortune, *amore*. We both love our son, and that is why we will make our marriage work this time,' Lucas answered, and she knew he was right. They were where they were because they had to be, but maybe time, the great healer, would restore something of what had been lost.

The remainder of the journey passed pleasantly enough, with Lucas pointing out various sites of interest when the nightmare of a road allowed. It was hair-raising at times and Sofie was glad to get down it in one piece. They parked near the waterfront and walked along to where the market was a bustling place of noise and colour.

Lucas insisted on taking her hand in his and Sofie felt her heart lighten as they wandered around the stalls that seemed to carry everything under the sun. Making herself understood was no problem as she spoke very good French, having been good at languages at school. There were so many bargains that, by the time they were ready to have a late lunch, they were loaded down with parcels. Lucas decided to take them back to the car, leaving Sofie to wait in the shade for him to return.

It was whilst she was doing so that her eye was caught by a man standing in the shadows over by the harbour wall. He looked alarmingly familiar, although he was half turned away from her, and her heart kicked as she sat up straighter to get a better look. In build and colouring, he reminded her of Gary Benson, and shock tore through her like lightning.

Of course it couldn't be him, she reassured herself, shielding her eyes to try and get a better look. She hadn't seen him since that day outside their house, before she'd left Lucas. She had almost forgotten all about him, in fact, with all that had happened. In England he might have turned up again eventually, but there was no way he could be here. And yet from this distance it looked very much like him. As if the man sensed her attention, he turned his head and looked directly at her for a few mind-numbing seconds, before turning and walking away.

Feeling sick, Sofie shot to her feet. Her legs wanted to shake, but this time she refused to let them. That look had sent a chill through her, but she wasn't going to react to it. She had to remain in control because it *was* Gary Benson. Every instinct she possessed told her so. But she had to make sure. Had to know for certain.

Without another thought, she hastened after him, trying to close the distance between them without being seen. If the man wasn't Benson, and she prayed that he wasn't, she didn't want to be seen following him. Which was why, when he stopped some minutes later, she darted into a doorway and held her breath, heart racing like mad at the prospect of being discovered.

Immediately afterwards she felt like a complete idiot. What on earth was she doing? Creeping about like an inferior spy! She had to be crazy! But when, after a few seconds, she peeped round the wall and the street was empty, her nerves jolted violently. Where was he? Now she had to hurry down the street to the first junction and was fortunate enough to catch a glimpse of his back turning a corner further down that street. Unfortunately, by the time she reached that corner and looked round, he had vanished from sight.

Sofie sank back against the wall and took several steadying breaths. She'd lost him and now she would never know! She closed her eyes, the old familiar impotent anger roiling inside her. This couldn't be happening. How could he be here? How could he have known?

'The picture in the newspaper didn't do you justice, Sofie,' the voice that had haunted her down the years declared, and her eyes shot open to see Gary Benson standing mere feet away, smiling at her.

'Paper?' she queried, momentarily distracted from her anger.

'At the airport, behind that footballer,' Gary explained, and Sofie groaned silently, never having given the possibility of her being in the photograph a thought.

Gary laughed delightedly at her stunned expression. 'I know. It shook me, too. But as soon as I saw it, I knew I had to come and see you.'

'How did you find me?' The newspaper report would have said Nice, not this town.

'I looked up the name Antonetti in the local telephone book when I got here,' came the simple answer.

Sofie pushed herself upright and folded her arms angrily. 'This has got to stop, Gary. You cannot keep following me around and invading my life. I'm not interested in you. Can't you understand that?'

As always, Gary merely shook his head in denial. 'I know you don't really mean that. We love each other. You know we do.'

Sofie stared at him and wanted to scream. How could life be so unfair? Every time she believed he was gone for good, he turned up to haunt her again. Well, she had had enough. Without thinking about the result of her actions, she took a step towards him and poked him in the chest.

'Go away, Gary, you little worm. I don't love you. Understand?' She poked him again to make sure he got the message. 'I love my husband. You are just a nasty little annoyance, and you know what happens to nasty little annoyances?' She poked him again, making him step backwards. 'They get stepped on, that's what! Now, go away and leave me alone!'

she ordered him coldly, then turned and walked away without a backward glance.

Gary Benson watched her go and he was no longer smiling.

Sofie felt remarkably buoyant after giving Gary Benson his marching orders. It felt good to have stood up for herself. Maybe she hadn't been as tactful as she might have been, but tact had got her nowhere in the past. A light-hearted laugh escaped her as she retraced her steps and she was so perked up it was some minutes before she realised Lucas would be wondering where she was. When she did, she stopped dead. How on earth was she going to explain her absence? she wondered. Maybe she wouldn't have to, though. She hadn't been gone that long. Maybe he hadn't returned yet.

However, the first person she saw when she got back to the place he had left her was Lucas. Hands on hips, he was scanning the crowd for her and, even at that distance, she could tell he was not happy. A few minutes later he spotted her and covered the distance between them in long, purposeful strides.

'Where on earth were you? I was beginning to get worried,' he declared, not unreasonably, and Sofie realised she should have thought of an answer before.

'I'm sorry,' she apologised swiftly, combing her hair away from her face with her fingers. 'I thought I saw someone I knew,' she said honestly, and wasn't at all surprised to see incredulity writ large upon his face.

'Here? You thought you saw someone you knew, here?'

She shrugged and spread her hands. 'It's not as crazy as it sounds. This is a holiday area, after all,' she pointed out reasonably.

'OK, I take your point,' he conceded. 'So, who was it?'

Sofie pulled a face, abandoning the truth. 'That's the

problem, I never got close enough to make sure.' She didn't want to talk about Gary Benson now. She just wanted him to go away and leave her alone.

Lucas's eyebrows rose. 'Who did you think it was?'

'Oh, just someone from the past. You wouldn't know him,' she dismissed the whole thing—or thought she had.

'Him?' Lucas queried rather sharply and, when she looked at him, his eyes had narrowed.

Amazed, and rather pleased, by these signs of male suspicion, Sofie laughed. 'There's no need to be jealous. It wasn't that kind of relationship,' she told him lightly, expecting he would move on, but he remained rooted to the spot.

'Just what kind of relationship was it, exactly?' he persisted, folding his arms across his chest and sticking to the subject like chewing-gum on a shoe.

Sofie widened her eyes at him, hardly believing what she was hearing. Her heart, though, was beating just a little faster. 'A one-sided one. On his part, not mine. Look, can we please drop the subject? I'm hungry. Can we go and eat now?'

'Are you sure that's all it was?'

She had joked about him being jealous, but he was giving a first rate impression of being just that. 'Of course I'm sure.'

One eyebrow quirked her way. 'Then why did you go after him?'

The question floored her, because obviously she wouldn't have wanted to go in search of someone she didn't like. She had to think fast. 'Because I wanted to make sure it wasn't him. I didn't want his presence spoiling our visit. Anyway, why does it bother you so much?'

He moved then, and his expression became shuttered. 'It doesn't. I was just curious. Let's eat,' he said, with a complete about-face, and gently turned her in the direction of the restaurant he had in mind.

Sofie's mind was buzzing as they ate the delicious food. Could he really be jealous? Did that mean he still cared for her? More to the point, if he did, how did that make her feel? He was still the same man who had betrayed her, so could she trust him with her heart? Dared she? She honestly didn't know, but she knew she wasn't going to dismiss the possibility. Only a fool would do that, and she wasn't a fool.

They spent the rest of the day strolling along the beach, finding a comfortable place to sit and simply lying back and watching the world go by. Finally they drove back to the villa in the late afternoon. Tom came running out of the house as they drew up and seeing him brought a smile to her lips and a glow to her heart. She jumped from the car and met him halfway, dropping to her knees to enfold him in her arms.

'Hey, Mum! Mummy, you're strangling me!' Tom protested moments later, wriggling in her arms, and she was forced to let him go.

'Sorry, darling,' she apologised, ruffling his hair. 'I missed you.'

'I missed you, too,' Tom responded brightly. 'We built this really great race track. Come and see it,' he urged her and, before she could say anything, he had turned and run back inside.

Sofie folded her arms and stared after him with a rueful sigh. A hand under her arm made her glance up to see Lucas staring down at her, his eyes dancing with amusement.

'I take it he was more interested in cars than you?' he teased as he helped her to her feet.

Sofie sent him a wry smile. 'Children want you when they want you, but at other times you're just a mother making a fuss,' she explained, and he smiled back at her.

'That I'm beginning to understand,' he said wryly, and Sofie looked deeply into his eyes.

'I really do love him so very much,' she told him. 'More than you could ever imagine.'

Lucas ran a gentle hand down her cheek. 'I believe you, *caro*. I have a very good imagination.'

When Sofie smiled, he slipped his arm around her waist. 'Come on. Let's go see this amazing track Tom's talking about,' he suggested and, for once in complete accord, they walked inside together.

CHAPTER TEN

THAT night they made love with a new depth of intensity. Sofie couldn't explain why, but it seemed as if both of them needed the other's passion, not their gentleness. If either was startled by the tempestuousness of the other's response, that was soon forgotten. Their bed became a battlefield where first one, then the other attempted to inflict the most pleasure. It was wild and hot, and their slick bodies writhed together over the silken sheets. Every sense was heightened by raw sensuality. Each kiss and caress drew forth a gasp, moan or sigh of rapture.

Passion burnt too hot and too fast to last long, and yet by sheer strength of will they managed to draw the moment out until, eventually, need overcame them. Consumed by desire, they came together in a soul-shattering moment of the purest pleasure either had ever known. It left them drained yet most beautifully replete, and they fell asleep in each other's arms.

Hours later, Sofie stirred. It was early, judging by the amount of light coming in through the window. Turning her head, she could see Lucas lying beside her, face down, arms and legs spread-eagled. There was the blue-black shadow of beard on his chin, and one curl of hair had dropped over his forehead, but he was still the most beautiful man she had ever seen. Despite everything that had happened between them, she could never regret knowing him, and would love him until the end of time.

Not wanting to wake him, she gently rolled off the bed and reached for her robe. Padding into the bathroom, she showered and washed her hair, towelling it dry before slipping on her robe again and returning to the bedroom. Lucas was still asleep, so she curled up in a chair by the window and watched the sunrise.

When it came, it was as beautiful as their lovemaking, filling her heart with longing for things to stay just the way they were. She wanted them to be a family. A happy, loving family, and nothing bad could ever touch them. Of course, that wasn't always possible when you lived in the real world, but it would be wonderful.

It was a nice dream, Sofie thought, and sighed wistfully.

'Why so pensive, *caro?*' Lucas's question drew her gaze back to the bed, where he was now on his side, head resting on his hand as he watched her.

'I was just daydreaming,' she responded, smiling, her eyes running over him, enjoying the rugged figure he portrayed.

'What about?' he challenged, one eyebrow raised. 'You're not thinking of leaving me again, are you?'

The softly voiced remark tore through her system with all the savagery of a tornado. The vehemence of her response told her, as nothing else could, that she would never leave Lucas again of her own free will. If he told her to go, that would be different, but her heart knew she was where she was supposed to be—for good or ill. 'No! How could you even think that?' she asked, unable to keep a tremor from her voice, for he had shaken her badly.

Lucas looked amazingly calm. 'Because last night we made love the same way we did before you left me.'

Sofie sat up, her mouth forming a perfect circle of surprise. 'That was the night before you went away on business. I knew I wasn't going to see you for days!'

Sitting up, Lucas swung his legs to the floor, bringing him that much closer to where she sat in the chair. 'That's right, and those days turned into weeks, then months, then years. It's not something I'm likely to forget.'

She shook her head in swift denial. 'That was then. I have no intention of leaving you now. The situation isn't the same. You're imagining things.'

He looked at her steadily, then shrugged. 'I hope so,' he said dryly, standing and stretching before walking over to the bathroom door. There he paused and glanced back over his shoulder. 'Because it's hard to love someone who keeps disappearing,' he added with a smile, and disappeared into the bathroom.

Sofie stared after him, stunned, but, as it wore off, she was galvanised into action. Jumping from the chair, she hurried after him. In the bathroom, Lucas was just stepping into the shower, but for once she wasn't sidetracked by the beautiful male body.

'What do you mean?' she charged him. 'You don't love me!'

One eyebrow lifted. 'I don't? It feels like I do,' he argued as he slid the shower door shut.

Sofie was momentarily rooted to the spot. Was she dreaming? Surely he couldn't really be saying… Needing confirmation, she crossed the room and opened the shower door. Steam billowed out and she waved it away with her hand.

'If this is supposed to be some kind of joke, I'm not laughing! You told me you stopped loving me years ago.'

Lucas was busily soaping himself, but he paused to look at her. 'I should have done, but I didn't. The truth is, I love you, *caro*. I always have and always will. Now, if you wouldn't mind, I'd like a bit of privacy.' With that, he reached out, pulled the door from her hand and shut it again.

Sofie was left to pace the room like a caged tiger. It wasn't that she didn't want to hear him say he loved her, but she simply didn't know if she could believe it. Trusting him came so hard after his affair. How could she believe him?

The water was turned off and the door opened. 'Still here?' Lucas queried ironically, taking a towel and drying himself off, finally draping it around his hips. 'What's bothering you, *caro?* Why can't I love you? It's hardly a crime.'

Realising her hands were shaking, she shoved them in the pockets of her robe. 'Because I ran away from you. Because I didn't tell you about Tom. Because you can't just throw it into the conversation like that. I only know you can't mean it, so take it back.'

Lucas shook his head, eyes gleaming. 'Can't. Won't,' he refused. Coming to stand in front of her, he put his hands on his hips. 'Now, what are you going to do?'

She stared at him helplessly, caught between wanting to believe him and not daring to. She didn't want to get hurt again. Dragging in a shaky breath, she glared at him. 'This isn't funny!'

He spread his hands. 'Am I laughing?'

Sofie pressed her lips together as they threatened to tremble. 'I don't need this!'

'OK, tell me what you do need,' he invited, and waited.

She stared back, unable to make her mouth form the words: *I need you.* Fear rose in her throat. Last time she had told him she loved him, he had betrayed her. What if he did it again? She was too afraid to take the risk. After a tense moment or two, she abruptly turned on her heel and went back into the bedroom. 'I need to get dressed,' she muttered to herself.

Lucas had followed her out and was leaning against the

doorjamb watching her. 'Don't you want to know what I would like you to do?'

'No,' she declared baldly, not sparing him a glance.

'I would like you to reciprocate,' he informed her, ignoring her response.

Sofie had to stop and look at him then. 'Reciprocate?'

Lucas nodded. 'Yes. You know. As in telling me you love me, too.'

Her heart jolted wildly and she could feel herself pale. 'I can't,' she retorted gruffly, looking back at the drawer she was searching, without any idea what she was looking for.

'Can't, *caro?* That's an interesting way of putting it,' he cajoled her, stepping closer. 'I already know you kept the ring I gave you. Tom tells me you keep a photo of us in your purse. You named our son after me. Would you do that if you felt nothing? Tell the truth and shame the devil, Sofie. Tell me you love me.'

An anger built of hurt and fear swelled inside her and she threw the clothes she was holding back in the drawer. 'Shut up!' she commanded, balling her hands into fists. 'I can't do it! Don't you understand that? I just can't.'

Lucas came to her then and caught her by the shoulders. 'Why not? Tell me, Sofie. Tell me why you can't.'

Tears glittered in her eyes like diamonds as she looked up at him. 'Because I'm afraid,' she admitted in a broken whisper, and saw him frown.

'Afraid? Afraid of what?'

Sofie shook her head, stepping back from the brink. 'Nothing. Nothing at all. Please, forget it.'

Lucas drew in an exasperated breath. 'My God, but you're stubborn! OK, have it your own way—for now,' he conceded, and stepped back, letting her go.

Sofie watched him sort out some clothes and start dressing. She felt so helpless because she ought to feel happy that he loved her, but her doubts wouldn't let her. 'I'm sorry,' she apologised softly and he gave her a quick glance.

'Don't be. You win some, you lose some. I'll go and look in on Tom whilst you get dressed. We'll meet you downstairs for breakfast,' he said with an offhand shrug. He paused on the way to the door to drop a kiss on her startled lips, then was gone.

Of course, the moment he left the strength went out of her legs and she had to sit on the bed to recover. Why did he have to tell her he loved her? It had been so much easier when she'd believed he didn't. Then she hadn't had to worry about him betraying her again. She had been able to push her fears into the background. His admission had brought everything back with a vengeance, and to give him the answer he wanted had been beyond her courage.

'Damn, damn, damn!' she muttered to herself as she finally got dressed. She didn't need things made any harder. Why couldn't he have left everything as it was?

Yet when, some fifteen minutes later, she went down to breakfast, dressed in shorts and a strappy top, she knew she looked cool and calm. Her insides might be churning, but at least it didn't show.

Lucas said he had some work to do after breakfast, so Sofie took Tom down to the pool by herself. They spent a couple of happy hours together, with Tom practising his doggy-paddle whilst she sat on the side. He splashed about, laughing, and chattering away nineteen to the dozen. Finally Sofie declared he had been in there long enough, so he climbed out and they played ball, until he got bored. Eventually he started to get hungry and he was happy to fall in with her suggestion that they should go back up to the house for lunch.

Eleanor was just coming out of the house as they reached it and, much to Sofie's surprise, she was looking a little concerned.

'What's wrong?' Sofie asked and the older woman wrung her hands anxiously.

'Nothing really. I'm sure everything's OK, it's only been fifteen minutes, but those cliffs are so dangerous,' she responded, not too clearly.

Sofie was lost. 'Why don't we sit down whilst you explain?' she suggested, and they all sat at the table. 'Now, tell me what happened.'

'Well,' Eleanor complied, clearly relieved to share her worries. 'It all started when a man came knocking at the door. He was quite distressed. Apparently his dog had fallen over the edge of the cliff and he had nothing to rescue it with. Naturally, I got Lucas, and he gathered up some rope and other things and went off with the man.'

Sofie suddenly had a sinking feeling in her stomach, though she couldn't have said why. 'Was it a local man?'

'No, he was English, and said he was a tourist. To be honest, he had a look about him that made me uneasy. Something about his eyes.'

Now Sofie understood her own reaction and her heart started to race. 'Tell me, was he about my height? Short brown hair and grey eyes?'

Eleanor's eyes opened wide. 'Why, yes. Do you know him?'

Did she know him? It had to be Gary Benson. She had no idea what he was doing, spinning a tale about a dog to Lucas, but she had a bad feeling about it. Her instinct told her she had to go after them, now.

'Yes, I believe I do. Eleanor, you have to look after Tom

for me. I'm going to go and find Lucas. Do you know where he keeps the keys to his car?' Sofie asked, thinking quickly and at the same time trying not to worry Eleanor or Tom.

Eleanor's expression said she sensed something, but didn't waste time asking. 'On him, probably. Take my car. The keys are on the tray by the door.'

Sofie got up hurriedly. 'Tom, be a good boy and stay with Nell.'

'OK, Mummy,' he replied, and his eyes were as big as saucers.

Sensing his worry, she gave him a smile. 'Don't worry. I won't be long. I'm only going to find Daddy and bring him home.'

There wasn't time for more, so she hurried through the house, finding the car keys with no trouble. At least Eleanor's car was small, as this would be the first time Sofie had driven on the other side of the road. Steering the vehicle on to the tarmac, she headed out along the way Eleanor had pointed.

'What are you up to, Gary?' she kept asking herself, unable to go as fast as she would have liked because of the strange car.

Mile after mile went by, and her tension was growing with every inch. Finally she rounded a bend and saw a car parked in a pull-off by the cliff-edge, with two men standing a little way along from it. She recognised them both, and her nerves leapt because they were standing far too close to the edge for her liking. Lucas was preparing a rope, whilst Gary was gesticulating over the side. Sofie gasped. Surely Lucas wasn't thinking of going over?

Pulling off the road, she jumped out of the car and hurried towards the two men. 'Lucas, please come away from the edge,' she urged him as she drew close. Just seeing him there made her distinctly nervous. She spared Gary a glance, and his face was consumed with annoyance.

'I'm fine, *amore*. Don't worry. I've done this before. This man's dog went over the edge. There's a ledge a short way down. It's probably on that. It won't take me a minute,' he responded, sending her a reassuring smile.

'I'm sure it won't, but there's one thing you should know. Gary doesn't have a dog, do you, Gary?' She shot the challenge at him, and he started as if he had been hit.

Lucas's head came up and round. 'Who? What?' he asked, looking first at Sofie, then at the other man. Something he saw there made him drop the rope. 'What's going on? Who is this man?'

'His name is Gary Benson,' Sofie explained, walking a little closer to him. 'He's been stalking me for years. Whenever I think he's gone, he turns up again, turning my life into a nightmare.'

Lucas's brows rose as he instantly made the connection. 'He was the man in the market yesterday?'

Before Sofie could do more than nod, Gary Benson closed the gap between them. He was almost beside himself with rage. 'Damn you, Sofie! How could you do this? I loved you! I sent you the photographs so you would dump him! You can't love him!'

Shock tore through her at what she heard and she turned to him. '*You* sent me the pictures? Oh, my God! I never even suspected!'

Lucas stepped forward. 'Hold on a minute. What photographs?'

Gary laughed, and there was an edge of madness in it. 'Photos of you with another woman! They were supposed to make her stop loving you! I thought she had when she left you, but she just goes back to you every time! Can't she see you're not worth it? Can't she see I love her more than you do?'

Sofie shook her head, feeling sick. 'He *is* worth it. He *does* love me. And, what's more, I love him!' she declared, looking at Gary Benson with utter distaste. 'You're despicable. What were you trying to do, bringing Lucas out here?'

Lucas smiled grimly. 'If I'm not mistaken, *amore,* I think he intended to shove me over this cliff.'

Gary Benson didn't even pretend to lie. 'Yes, and I would have done it if she hadn't come along and interfered.'

Lucas held out his hand towards Sofie. 'I think it's time we left, *caro,*' he said firmly.

Only too happy to agree, Sofie began to turn towards Lucas, and it was as she did so that all hell broke loose. She heard the sound of rushing feet behind her and saw the look of alarm on her husband's face, then an arm caught her around the waist, knocking the air out of her.

From a distance she could hear Gary Benson's voice crying out, 'No! If I can't have her, neither can you!'

Seconds later she could feel herself heading towards the edge of the cliff. She fell, hitting the ground and rolling, Gary's arm still around her. Then there was a strangled cry of fear and she felt the lower half of her body swing out into space before bending down under the pull of Gary's weight.

She never knew if she said Lucas's name, or just thought she did, but in that same instant two strong hands grasped her by the wrists and held on tightly. She looked up, and there was Lucas, lying stretched out on the ground, using all his strength to stop her sliding over the cliff after Gary. Then Gary must have lost his grip as she felt him frantically searching for something to hold, but it was too late. His weight disappeared from her legs and, as Lucas quickly pulled her away from danger, they could hear Gary's scream as he fell, followed, moments later, by deathly silence.

Sofie scrambled over to Lucas, flinging her arms around his neck and holding on tight as she began to shake with reaction. His arms fastened around her like a vice, as if he would never let her go.

'Don't you know you should never go anywhere with strange men?' she cried into his shoulder, and felt Lucas shudder.

'The man was mad,' he declared thickly. 'He would have killed us all, but instead he only killed himself.'

She went still. 'Then, he's dead?' she asked, easing back so that she could see Lucas's face.

'Nothing could survive that drop,' he confirmed solemnly, then closed his eyes for a moment. 'For one awful moment, I thought you were going over too,' he said in a choked voice, and she could see the faintest gleam of moisture under his closed lashes.

Instantly she pressed a kiss to each eye. 'But you saved me. I'm still here,' she whispered, and Lucas opened his eyes, smiling at her.

'Yes, you're still here,' he agreed, framing her head with his hands and looking deeply into her eyes. 'If you had gone over, I would have died, too. You are my life, *amore.*'

Sofie drew in a ragged breath, her lips trembling as tears started to her eyes. 'I know. And you are mine. I love you.' Suddenly they were the easiest three words to say.

His smile broadened and he laughed huskily. 'You chose the strangest place to tell me. I want to kiss you, but I think we're about to be rescued ourselves,' he added, and in the distance they could hear the sound of sirens heading their way.

It turned out that a passing motorist had witnessed the incident and had telephoned the police and rescue services. There were a lot of questions and explanations over the following few hours but, at the end of it, Lucas and Sofie were allowed to go home. Lucas had phoned ahead to tell his grand-mother that they were both all right, which was all Tom needed to know. He was waiting outside for them when Lucas finally drove them home in Eleanor's car.

'Mummy! Daddy! Did you hear the police cars?' he shouted excitedly, and Lucas swept him up into his arms.

'We sure did,' he responded, tickling him until he was gig-gling. 'There was an accident along the road,' he added, ex-changing a knowing look with Sofie over their son's head.

'Did the man find his dog?' Tom persisted, and Sofie reached up to brush hair out of his eyes.

'The dog was OK, darling. Everything is OK now,' she told him, and hoped that it was, for she knew she still had a lot of explaining to do. Which was why she turned to Eleanor. 'Would you mind looking after Tom again? I want to talk to Lucas.'

'Not at all. We have great plans for a new race track. Come along, Tom. Let's see if we can't make it super-duper.' She held out her hand to him and when Lucas set him down he went off happily with the old lady.

'So,' Lucas said, when they were alone, 'where do you want to start?'

Sofie drew in a deep breath. 'Let's walk this way,' she sug-gested, and they slowly began to walk down through the garden. After a while they found a seat in a sheltered spot and sat down on it, whilst Sofie tried to get her thoughts in order.

'Why didn't you tell me about this man… Gary?' Lucas asked after a while, and she shook her head sadly.

'Gary Benson. I said nothing because I thought he had gone. He'd been stalking me since I met him in college, and would come and go. I'd not seen him until he turned up in one of our wedding photos.'

'Ah,' Lucas said softly. 'Yes, I remember.'

Sofie quickly told him about Gary turning up at the house the same day, and how she had sent him off. 'He was angrier than I'd ever seen him but, when I saw nothing more of him, I thought he had finally taken the hint.' She paused and took a deep breath. 'Then, whilst you were away, the photos arrived.'

Lucas sat up straighter, turning in his seat so he could watch her. 'The photos of me with another woman?'

She nodded. 'I had no idea Gary had sent them. I thought it was just someone at your office who had a grudge against you,' she explained, meeting his eyes and seeing the concern there. 'I didn't want to believe it.'

'So why did you? I take it the photos were the reason you ran away. Why didn't you ask me, *caro?*' He was mystified, and she could sense his hurt.

'Oh, but I did. I rang you. It was night where you were, and this woman answered. She had to get you out of bed, and she spoke to you as if she knew you very well. Intimately well. That was when I knew I had to go. I couldn't stay with a man who cheated on me, however much I loved him!'

Lucas looked thunderstruck and she could see the cogs working as memories were retrieved. 'That was you on the phone? We thought it was a prank call.'

Her heart contracted, even after all this time. 'We?'

'Laura was with me that night. She's my cousin's wife. They couldn't make it to the wedding but, when they heard I was in the city, they came to see me. I put them up for the night, in the suite I had booked. They had the bedroom and I had the couch. Laura heard the phone but I didn't. That was who you heard, *caro,* and if you had stayed on the line I would have told you so.'

Sofie went hot and cold as it dawned on her that she had abandoned Lucas and their marriage for nothing. 'Oh, God!

I'm so sorry. I thought… I really thought… But I should have known better. I loved you. I should have clung on to that.'

Lucas moved closer, putting his arm around her shoulder, though she resisted. Not that she didn't want him to hold her, she just couldn't imagine how he could after what she had said. 'Why didn't you?' he asked seconds later, and she sighed.

'Because I felt betrayed. It goes back a long way with me, Lucas. I thought Gary was a nice man, but he turned out to be a sick individual. It destroyed my trust in men. I kept thinking they would turn out to be like him. Until I met you. You made me start trusting again, but it wasn't easy. I was still strengthening the walls when the photos came along, and they knocked them down. They made me believe you had done what I always expected you would—betray me and break my trust. I couldn't live with that again, Lucas, even though I loved you. How could I ever have trusted you again?'

A long sigh of understanding left him as he drew her closer, holding her tight. 'Now I understand. What can I say? I went out with many women before I met you, but none since then. Who that woman was, and how Benson got hold of the photos, I have no idea.'

Sofie groaned. 'And I should never have trusted those photos over you!' she bewailed her own insecurity, which made Lucas smile gently.

'You couldn't help yourself, *caro*. Anyone can see that. Trust is fragile, especially when you love someone. When our happiness depends on someone else, we are all treading on thin ground. But we can change that, *amore*.'

She looked up at him then, wondering what he meant. 'How?'

'By believing in what we feel for each other. I make you a promise, here and now, that I will never knowingly betray your trust in me. I love you. I may have lost sight of it for a while, but the truth is that I always have and always will love you, *amore*.' He spoke with such a depth and wealth of emotion that it made her heart swell.

Her smile was watery. 'I never stopped loving you, Lucas. I was just so afraid of being betrayed again. I want to trust you.'

'You can. Forget the past. You were made to believe lies, but without that you would have kept on trusting me. If your love is strong enough, the trust will come back. Only believe in us, *caro*.'

Sofie flung her arms around his neck. 'It is. I do. I just don't know how you can forgive me for putting us through six years of misery.'

He laughed huskily. 'How can I not, when I love you? Gary Benson is gone. He cannot make any more mischief. We're free to live our lives the way we wish. Do you know what I want?'

She shook her head, smiling at last, knowing the dark cloud had gone from their lives. 'No.'

'I want to live the rest of my life loving you,' he told her, all the pent-up emotion he felt making his voice thick and husky.

'And Tom,' she said, equally huskily, and he laughed.

'And Tom, and all his brothers and sisters.'

Sofie blinked. 'How many were you planning on?'

Now he grinned that wolfish grin she loved so much. 'Oh, a round figure. Four. Six, maybe. What do you think?'

She laughed, a happy sound that echoed across the garden. 'I think I love you, Lucas Antonetti.'

THE ROYAL HOUSE OF NIROLI

...International affairs, seduction and passion guaranteed

VOLUME FOUR

The Tycoon's Princess Bride
by Natasha Oakley

Isabella Fierezza has always wanted to make a difference to the lives of the people of Niroli and she's thrown herself into her career. She's about to close a deal that will ensure the future prosperity of the island. But there's just one problem...

Domenic Vincini: born on the neighbouring, *rival* island of Mont Avellana, and he's the man who can make or break the deal. But Domenic is a man with his own demons, who takes an instant dislike to the perfect Fierezza princess...

Worse, Isabella can't be in the same room with him – without wanting him! But if she gives in to temptation, she forfeits her chance of being queen...and will tie Niroli to its sworn enemy!

Available 5th October 2007

M&B

THE ROYAL HOUSE OF NIROLI

*...International affairs, seduction
and passion guaranteed*

VOLUME FIVE

Expecting His Royal Baby
by Susan Stephens

Nico Fierezza: as an internationally successful
magnate, he's never needed to rely on his family's
royal name. But now he's back – and the King has
matched him with a suitable bride. Niroli is ready
to welcome its new ruler!

Carrie Evans has been in love with Nico, her
boss, for years. But, after one magical night of loving,
he ruthlessly discarded her...and now she's
discovered she's carrying his child!

*Everything is in place for Nico's forthcoming nuptials.
But there's an unexpected wedding guest: Carrie, who is
willing to do anything to protect the future of her baby...
The question is – does anything include marrying Nico?*

Available 2nd November 2007

www.millsandboon.co.uk

M&B

4 FREE

BOOKS AND A SURPRISE GIFT!

We would like to take this opportunity to thank you for reading this Mills & Boon® book by offering you the chance to take FOUR more specially selected titles from the Modern™ series absolutely FREE! We're also making this offer to introduce you to the benefits of the Mills & Boon® Reader Service™—

- ★ FREE home delivery
- ★ FREE gifts and competitions
- ★ FREE monthly Newsletter
- ★ Exclusive Reader Service offers
- ★ Books available before they're in the shops

Accepting these FREE books and gift places you under no obligation to buy, you may cancel at any time, even after receiving your free shipment. Simply complete your details below and return the entire page to the address below. You don't even need a stamp!

YES! Please send me 4 free Modern books and a surprise gift. I understand that unless you hear from me, I will receive 6 superb new titles every month for just £2.89 each, postage and packing free. I am under no obligation to purchase any books and may cancel my subscription at any time. The free books and gift will be mine to keep in any case.

P7ZED

Ms/Mrs/Miss/Mr ....Initials ....
BLOCK CAPITALS PLEASE

Surname ....

Address ....

....

....Postcode..................................

Send this whole page to:
UK: FREEPOST CN81, Croydon, CR9 3WZ